Christmas Mystery!

"I'm sorry," Ryan's mother said as he emerged into the kitchen and gave her the jelly jar, "but now I need a jar of raspberry jelly, too. Could you run back down and get one?"

Like I could say no… Ryan went down into the basement again. As he walked to the shelves with the jars of preserves, he noticed something had changed.

The old locked door. The door that hadn't been opened in nearly seventy years.

Although nobody had been in the basement in the barely one minute since he had last been here, the door now had a Christmas wreath on it.

And it was no longer old and battered, with faded and peeling paint. It looked new and freshly painted.

Puzzled, Ryan went over to take a closer look.

As he approached, he could faintly hear something from the other side of the door. Voices. Lots of them. And music. Christmas music.

In a room that had been sealed for close to seven decades?

Something very strange was afoot here. Almost without thinking, he reached out and wrapped his fingers around the doorknob. For almost seventy years, the door had been locked tight. But now the knob turned easily.

The door opened...

128 West Fairground Street.
1895.

In Time for Christmas

Dwight R. Decker

Vesper Press

Northlake, IL

Cover by SelfPubBookCovers.com/ RLSather
Illustration on page 100 by Alan Fletcher Bradford
Interior illustrations are original or in the public domain

Some names of celebrities and commercial properties mentioned in passing are used for purposes of verisimilitude without endorsement or authorization by their respective owners. No effect or claim on trademark or ownership status is intended or should be inferred.

Song lyrics quoted in "Christmas Carol Critique" were obtained from various sites on the Internet. Some of the songs are very old and in the public domain. Newer ones still under copyright are cited here for the purpose of criticism and comment in accordance with the Fair Use doctrine.

Earlier versions of "In Time for Christmas," "A Hard Day's Flight," and "Christmas Carol Critique" were published in low-circulation fanzines or as Christmas mailings to family and friends.

*V*Vesper Press

Northlake, Illinois

ISBN: 1979736715
ISBN-13: 978-1979736718

Contents

Dedication

For Wayne, Alan, and Morgan,
who could have had an adventure like this.

In Time for Christmas

Introduction

Some years ago, I had the idea of writing a Christmas story to send out with my cards at Yuletide for the possible amusement if not amazement of my family and friends.

The inspiration came from seeing the movie *The Polar Express*. I had some mistaken notion that the kids on the train had been gathered from different eras (I was overthinking some things that were probably just inconsistencies). Then I thought, why not actually *do* a Christmas party with kids from different eras?

So I began writing, and soon it became obvious that the initial premise of a cross-time Christmas party wasn't enough by itself. Something had to *happen*, and the word count kept expanding as I added new incidents and scenes. The first year's Christmas came and went with the story still unfinished and the title, "In Time for Christmas," became something of a joke. The story ended up taking years to write and it wasn't in time for *three* consecutive Christmases.

Eventually, it was finally finished just as another Christmas was around the corner. I photocopied it in fanzine format at what was then Kinko's, collated and stapled it, and sent it out to the mailing list. We will pass over the scream that resounded with the belated discovery that I had mistakenly referred to the hero by the wrong name in two paragraphs despite all the proofreading.

After that, the story languished in a box of my half-forgotten literary discards along with the unfinished fragments of abandoned projects. Since it actually was completed and because another Christmas is coming, I decided to rescue the story from obscurity and present it to the assembled multitude.

With a little luck, it might even be in time for *this* Christmas.

—DRD

In Time for Christmas

Chapter One

It was the Friday afternoon before Christmas and Mrs. Morton had given up on trying to do anything very serious in her 10th Grade English class. After passing out a list of books to read over the vacation, she let her students have the rest of the period free.

While some of the other kids got up from their seats and moved around the classroom to talk with each other, Ryan Thayer stayed at his desk. He pulled out a science-fiction novel he had borrowed from the library, a title most definitely not on Mrs. Morton's list of assigned reading, and thumbed to the bookmarked page where he had last left off. He had half an hour or so to wait before the bell rang, and it seemed like a good chance to get some reading done.

"Nerd!"

Ryan looked up, but he had already recognized the voice. A tallish, rather slender girl stood over him, looking down at the book in his hands with an expression of mild disdain. Her name was Kelsey and she was pretty enough in her way, with short, dark hair and large green eyes, but if Ryan had learned anything in this past school year, it was that even pretty girls came in all sorts, and some could be downright annoying. This one in particular.

"What's your problem?" he demanded, irritated.

"I'm not the one with the problem," she retorted. "You are." She gestured at the rest of the classroom. "Mrs. Morton gave us some free time but you've got your nose stuck in a book."

He glanced around. It wasn't like everyone in the room was engaged in unrestrained socializing. A couple of desks over, a boy was playing with a hand-held video game, and in other parts of the room at least two girls were texting on their phones.

"So what do you want me to do?" he asked a little peevishly.

"Well, you could talk to somebody."

"Who?"

There was a pause, as though Kelsey hadn't expected him to be so impossibly dense and she wasn't sure what to do next. "How about me?" she finally suggested. Then she shot her hand out to snatch Ryan's book away, as though she figured that without it he wouldn't have anything else to do but talk to her.

He saw her move coming and yanked the book out of her reach. "Hey, that's mine! What do you want?"

She hesitated, as though her self-confidence had suddenly faltered, then said, "There's going to be a Christmas parade downtown tonight and I thought... well, maybe I'd see you there..."

"I can't go, sorry. I've got some... er, stuff at home tonight." That was true to the extent that he planned to spend the evening in his room reading or watching a movie. It would be cold out that night, and he felt he had gotten a little old for something like a Christmas parade anyway. He turned back to where he had left off in the book.

"Well, if you can't, you can't..." Kelsey said, sounding almost a little hurt.

Two other girls joined Kelsey, her best friends April and Caitlin. Even though they were hardly anything alike, they hung out together so much that people called them the Trio.

"Just leave him be if he doesn't want to be halfway friendly," said Caitlin.

Now, if somebody had to pester him, why couldn't it be her? There was pretty, but then there was gorgeous. She was blonde and athletic, with both the cheerleaders and the girls' basketball team trying to recruit her. Just looking at Caitlin a couple of seats in front of him was dangerous for his concentration when the teacher was lecturing. Unfortunately, she was also dauntingly popular. Half the boys in the class had a crush on her and the other half just wouldn't admit it, so there was considerable competition there and his chances seemed fairly hopeless.

"Oh, I don't know..." said April in her soft, even melodious voice. "Sometimes a book can be a friend, too."

April usually didn't say much and what she had just said may have nearly doubled the number of words Ryan had heard her say since he first became aware of her, but she was smart, very pretty in a subtle way with long, dark hair, and it was mostly because of her that he sometimes found himself wishing he wouldn't be moving again at the end of the school year. And she had just come to his defense, too.

"It looks like these two are really close," Kelsey said, apparently including Ryan's book as one of the two, and sounding a little disgusted. "Let's go. I wouldn't want to get in the way of true friendship!" With some muffled giggles, the three scurried off.

What's her deal? Ryan wondered. It was bad enough that he had to sit next to Kelsey in English. Why did she have to keep pestering him? For some mysterious reason known only to her, she seemed to have made it her mission in life to get on his nerves. If only he could have arranged to sit next to one of the other two...

No point in worrying about it now. He turned back to his book and considered himself fortunate that he wasn't interrupted for the rest of the period.

When the bell rang, he felt a joyous relief. No more school until after New Year's. He grabbed his books, got up from his seat, and headed out of the classroom with the rest of the kids.

At fifteen, Ryan Thayer was of average height with an average build, an average brown-haired boy so average that he tended to get lost in a crowd. He sometimes even had trouble finding himself in class pictures. This was his first year in a Centerpoint school, and he had every expectation it would be his last. Once his father found a new job, the family would be moving again. Centerpoint was just a stopover, and everyone he met here this year would be left behind and probably soon forgotten.

Ryan stopped at his locker to get his coat, then left the building by way of the front lobby. On the way out, he passed a display case with historical odds and ends, like school newspapers, yearbooks, and pennants. Among the exhibits was a framed picture of a winning basketball team of long ago with his father in the line-up.

Cold air hit his face as he came outside. Though the sky was clear, snow covered the ground. A line of yellow school buses stood along the curb in front of the building, and he boarded the one that took him out to his neighborhood.

After a ten-minute ride through the streets of Centerpoint, Ryan got off at the convenience store on the corner of Main Street near his house to go the rest of the way on foot. He then turned down West Fairground Street, a wide avenue lined with bare trees and large old houses on both sides. Despite the name, any fairground that had ever been around here was long gone.

Along the way, he passed one of his neighbors on the sidewalk, a young mother named Mrs. Walton. Holding on tightly to her hand was

Connor, her two-year-old son, nearly spherical in his well-padded blue snowsuit. Ryan said hi and went on.

The big, rambling house at 128 dated back something like a century and a half. It had been in the family all that time, sheltering successive generations of Thayers. His grandparents owned it now, so it had been there when his father lost his job and needed a place to go while he made a fresh start. Even after several months of living in it, however, it still wasn't really home. His father didn't expect to stay here more than a year, so there was some reluctance to settle in. Ryan sometimes wished they could eventually go back to their old town where he had grown up and still had friends, but that didn't look like a realistic prospect.

It had been a little strange to move to Centerpoint and actually live in a town he already knew fairly well from family visits over the years. The Thayers went back a long way in Centerpoint, and he remembered hearing that the town was originally called Thayerville when it was just a village where the local farmers traded, somewhere out in the remote Midwestern cornfields. "Centerpoint" seemed to have been the result of the railroad coming through and putting a name on the station sign that served its own purposes.

Some of the family was still around, with a couple of cousins attending the local middle school and a second cousin in a grade school across town. Unfortunately, none of his relatives were the same age he was, so he'd had to start out the school year like any other new kid not knowing anybody in his classes at all.

The house was modestly decorated for Christmas, with just a wreath on the front door, plastic holly garland wrapped around the porch railing, and electric candles in the windows. Ryan went up the walk to the porch, passing Cody, his nine-year-old brother, who was already home from school and building a snowman in the front yard with a couple of his friends. In Ryan's view, little brothers were fairly useless in the grand scheme of things, but he was stuck with one and had to make the best of it.

As he came inside, Ryan glanced into the study just off the front hall. In an earlier day it had been called the parlor but now it was William Thayer Job-Hunting Central. Ryan saw his father sitting at a desk in front of a computer and checking job-listings. Mr. Thayer had read somewhere that the best way to look for a job was to make looking for a job itself a full-time job, and he had taken it to heart. He was a lean, wiry man approaching forty, with glasses and short-cropped hair that had been light to begin with and was now both turning gray and thinning on top. He looked so intent as he stared at the glowing screen that Ryan decided not to disturb him.

On the other side of the hall was the living room. Ryan's little sister, barely four, sat on the floor in front of the TV set engrossed in some cartoon or other, while his grandfather dozed in an easy chair, a newspaper on his chest. A large Christmas tree stood in a corner, decorated with a lot of heirloom ornaments Ryan remembered from Christmases past, and a low fire burned cozily in the fireplace.

Christmas itself was shaping up to be on the skimpy side this year, with his father out of work and his mother's hours cut at a job that didn't pay all that well to begin with. His grandparents were doing what they could to help, but even they were starting to look a bit strained with five additional people in the house. Ryan understood the situation and accepted it, though there were a few presents he wouldn't have minded finding under the tree. Books, mostly. His little brother, whose tastes ran more to expensive videogames, was having a harder time dealing with the bleak reality of diminished expectations.

He went upstairs to his room. Really upstairs, since it was on the third floor and technically a finished attic room. The pitch of the roof made the wall by his bed a little low, but this high up there was a great view out the windows, over the treetops and the roofs of neighboring houses and to the distant hills beyond. The one good thing about the move was that his grandparents' house had enough spare rooms that he could have one of his own rather than having to share it with his brother. He hadn't been there long enough to really personalize it, so the room still looked a little empty and unlived-in, with some still unpacked boxes of books spilling out of the closet.

He dropped his coat and textbooks off on his bed. The one cloud in the otherwise sunny sky of nearly two straight weeks of freedom was a few too many teachers who thought a winter break was just an empty space that needed to be filled with assigned books to read, reports to write, and pages of Geometry problems to solve. Then he went back downstairs with the idea of getting a snack before doing anything else.

In the kitchen, his mother was working on getting dinner ready, and she was just then looking in the refrigerator for something. She was about forty, her hair turning to gray, with glasses. She had looked a little stressed these past few months, as though the move and change in circumstances had been harder on her than anyone else.

"Oh, Ryan," she said when she saw him, "we're almost out of strawberry jelly. Could you go down and get another jar?"

"Sure," he replied with a shrug. It wasn't like he had anything better to do. Even so, he noticed he felt just a touch reluctant to go down into the basement. For that matter, his mother had sounded apologetic for asking him to do it, as though she felt the same reluctance herself. No wonder, since it was a spooky basement.

The cellar door was just off the kitchen. Making his way down the bare wooden stairs, he remembered being afraid to go down there when he was younger and visiting his grandparents. Especially at night. For a little kid, it had been the stuff of nightmares inspired by scary movies. Once he'd had a dream of being lost in some vast, dark, and empty place that was half castle dungeon and half endless cavern, with who knew what monsters lurking in the shadows, and when he woke up he realized that it had been an exaggerated impression of the basement. Now that he was older, he could see it as just the ordinary basement it was, with dirty concrete block walls, a bare and dusty cement floor, wooden beams high overhead and thick with cobwebs, and only a very few naked light bulbs that seemed more useful for casting deep shadows in corners than illuminating anything, but some of the old fear still lingered at the back of his mind.

Scattered here and there was the accumulated junk of generations. When a baby carriage had lost a wheel, this was where it ended up, perhaps with some idea of fixing it eventually, but forty years later it was still here, coated in dust that had never been disturbed. There were even some ancient-looking wooden barrels that wouldn't have been out of place in some old-time general store. The sole concession to modernity was the electric furnace, which had replaced a coal-burning iron monstrosity long before Ryan's time.

Along one wall were some wooden shelves. Since Grandma Thayer was old-fashioned enough to like "putting up preserves," as she called it, and since the basement was relatively cool even in the summer, this was where the jars of various kinds of homemade fruit jelly were kept in orderly rows. Ryan found one with "Strawberry" neatly lettered on a glued paper label on the side and picked it off the shelf. As he turned to go, something in the opposite wall caught his eye: a closed and rather solid-looking wooden door with faded and peeling paint.

One of the house's minor mysteries was what was behind that battered old door. Ryan's mental picture of the house's overall floorplan suggested a room of some size, and when he was younger he had liked to imagine all kinds of wonderful things hidden away inside. Treasure chests overflowing with gold coins and jewelry, or perhaps a toy train layout built long ago...

The reality was probably fairly disappointing. While the key to the door was now hopelessly lost, Ryan's grandfather said he had seen it opened once, when he was a very little boy. His memory was faded, but Grandpa recalled that the room was mostly empty. There was a family story that some umpty-great uncle had been seized as a high-school student by an enthusiasm for chemistry and set up a home laboratory in that room until the other relatives grew tired of the smoke and smells. Fearing that it was only a question of what he would do first — burn the house down or blow it up — they made him dismantle the equipment. Whether the junk in the room had been the remnants of the laboratory, Grandpa couldn't say, though he had some impression of glassware that might have been dusty old beakers and test tubes.

The one thing he did remember clearly was a very old bicycle in a corner, the kind with an enormously high front wheel that Ryan had only seen in pictures. The front wheel of this one was badly twisted, though, the result of some long-ago accident. The old high-wheelers were hard to ride, Grandpa had explained, which was why more modern bicycles with smaller wheels of equal size had first been marketed in the late 19th Century as "safety" bicycles.

Otherwise, with the key missing, Grandpa doubted if the door could be opened without breaking it down. The only other access would have been through the one small window that had once let a meager amount of light into the room, but it could be seen from the outside foundation that even that had long since been bricked over. From what Grandpa remembered of what was inside the room, breaking in probably wouldn't be worth the trouble, whether for the sake of curiosity or for the more practical reason of looking for antiques that might have some value.

Whatever mysteries lay behind the door wouldn't be solved by just standing there and looking at it, and Ryan turned and went back upstairs.

"I'm sorry," his mother said as he emerged into the kitchen and gave her the jelly jar, "but now I need a jar of raspberry jelly, too. Could you run back down and get one?"

Like I could say no… Ryan went down into the basement again. As he walked to the shelves with the jars of preserves, he noticed something had changed.

The old locked door.

Although nobody had been in the basement in the barely one minute since he had last been here, the door now had a Christmas wreath on it.

And it was no longer old and battered, with faded and peeling paint. It looked new and freshly painted.

Puzzled, Ryan went over to take a closer look.

As he approached, he could faintly hear something from the other side of the door. Voices. Lots of them. And music. Christmas music.

In a room that had been sealed for close to seven decades?

Something very strange was afoot here. Almost without thinking, he reached out and wrapped his fingers around the doorknob. For nearly

9

seventy years, the door had been locked tight. But now the knob turned easily.

The door opened.

Inside, there was a party going on.

Chapter Two

The room, supposedly empty except for some random dust-covered debris, was now clean, brightly lit, lavishly decorated for Christmas, and filled with kids. Everyone was laughing and talking while Christmas music played from seemingly out of nowhere. There weren't any visible speakers, anyway. Some familiar odors hit Ryan's nose, a mixture of pine scent and baking cookies.

Standing by the doorway was a tall and rather stout elderly man with a spectacular white mustache and wearing a tailed jacket, a vest with a watch chain, and a tied ribbon-type tie.

"You must be Ryan," he said festively in a deep, almost booming voice. "We've been waiting for you. Well, don't just stand there! Come on in and join the party!"

"Er... who are you?" Ryan asked as he tentatively stepped into the room.

"Your Uncle Gadwell, but that's not important. Come in, come in! Have some punch, make some friends. It's a party, so have fun!"

As he stepped into the room and Uncle Gadwell closed the door behind him, Ryan tried to think. There had been some mention in family circles of an Uncle Gadwell somewhere, but never in connection with anyone who was alive. At least not in this century.

Ryan looked around. The kids ranged somewhat in age, with some maybe as young as ten and others around sixteen. What struck him was that they weren't all dressed the same way. One boy carefully ladling an orange-colored drink from the punchbowl into a glass was wearing a black velvet suit with white lace cuffs. Next to him, grabbing some cookies off a tray, was a boy with a short hairstyle Ryan knew was called a crewcut, wearing jeans, high-top tennis shoes, and a checked flannel shirt. Nearby, two girls were talking, one wearing a bonnet and a floor-length gingham dress that made her look as though she had wandered in from Center-point's Pioneer Days celebration, except that wouldn't be until summer. The other girl had very short hair with a tuft in front surprisingly similar to that one boy's crewcut and wore a one-piece red jumpsuit made out of something shimmery and shiny, with a wide white belt and white boots that went a little above her ankles, along with a band around her left wrist that seemed more high tech than just a watch.

"Is this a costume party?" Ryan asked a little uncertainly. "I'm afraid I don't have a costume..."

Uncle Gadwell chuckled. "Oh no, you're fine! It's a come as you are party." He turned away to attend to something else.

Ryan took another look around. The room was decorated with garlands hanging from the ceiling and on the walls, interspersed with wreaths, boughs of holly, and bunches of poinsettias. Some mistletoe was hanging at the other end of the room, but the kids seemed to be well aware of it and were careful to avoid it. A plump middle-aged woman, perhaps Uncle Gadwell's wife, in an antique-looking dress with puffed sleeves and an apron was just then replenishing some of the cookie dishes from a metal tray she held in an oven-gloved hand. A couple of doors in one wall led to a small kitchen and possibly a bathroom. That last would be a good thing to have available with something like fifteen kids on hand for an extended period.

He spotted two kids talking in a corner. One was wearing clothes not too different from Ryan's, but the other had a shaved head and wore a blue tunic over some sort of silvery bodysuit that seemed to move in ways that didn't match the movements of the body within, like a living outer skin with a mind of its own.

Ryan couldn't hear what they were saying, but Silver Suit seemed to be demonstrating his outfit's capabilities to the amazed other boy, like a pocket that was there when he needed it and not there when he didn't. Then Silver Suit gestured as though inviting the other boy to hit him in the stomach. Reluctant at first, the other boy finally let fly, seemingly saying, "Well, if you insist..."

The boy's fist just bounced off with no apparent effect on the target. He took a step back, clutching his fist as though with suddenly bruised knuckles, as though the suit had somehow seen the fist coming and instantly hardened itself at the likely point of impact. He didn't look angry, however, and seemed more amazed and impressed. Both boys laughed, evidently enjoying the whole thing.

If that one girl's red jumpsuit had seemed high tech, the silver suit seemed even higher techier. *What store out at the mall carries that? It looks like the latest thing.* A hundred years from now. On Mars.

On the other side of the room, an open archway led into another room, not as brightly lit. Exactly what purpose the second room served, Ryan couldn't tell from where he stood, but its function was less puzzling than the mere fact of its existence. If the room he was in corresponded to the locked room in the basement beneath his house, the adjoining room would be somewhere beyond the walls and under the side yard. And Ryan could see another door on the other side of that room. Was there a whole underground complex beneath the yards and houses of his neighborhood? That nobody even knew about? He had a feeling there was more to it than that.

Giving up trying to figure it out, Ryan looked among the kids for someone he might know, but came up empty. It wasn't surprising, since he was new in school this year and didn't know all that many of the local kids yet. Even so, some of the kids here did seem to have some hazy familiarity. Like that girl in the red jumpsuit.

She noticed him staring at her and turned away from the long-dressed girl to look at him quizzically. Now that he saw her face from the front, he realized that he didn't know her after all. And yet... she reminded him of someone.

"Er..." Ryan stumbled. "Sorry, I thought you were somebody I knew." *Now she probably thinks I'm a complete idiot.*

Actually, she just seemed more baffled. "I could say the same thing about you," she said. "But I'm sure we've never met."

"No, I don't think we have," Ryan agreed.

Red Jumpsuit shrugged and turned back to the girl in gingham, as though she preferred to leave the status of their acquaintance at having never met and pretending the conversation had never happened.

As long as he was here... Ryan ladled a glass of punch from the big bowl for himself. Sipping it, he decided it was probably a mix of 7-Up and fruit juice, but there was a spicy tang to it that he couldn't quite put his finger on.

He noticed he was standing next to a beefy boy in shorts and suspenders, horizontally striped shirt, limp socks drooping around his ankles, and scuffed brown shoes with laces, who was attacking the cookie dishes as though he had been starving for a week. Something about the kid seemed familiar to Ryan, but it took a moment to place him since this was real life and in color. The boy reminded him of some cast member or other in an ancient comedy series he had seen on the retro TV cable channel about a gang of kids in the 1930s.

A rather chubby boy on the other side of Ryan then decided to strike up a conversation.

"You look pretty normal," he said. "Any idea what's going on and who all these kids in the costumes are?"

Dwight R. Decker

This boy was dressed about the same way he was, in jeans and shirt, though his hair was a tad longer. Then Ryan noticed his shoes, which weren't like any he had seen before. More like aerodynamic running shoes designed using a wind tunnel for gods who ran at 200 miles an hour.

"You don't know any more about it than I do?" Ryan asked, though it was more of a statement of disappointment than a question.

"Nah, I'm not even sure how I got here," the kid said. "One second I was in my house and then here I was. Wherever here is."

"I thought this was the basement of my own house," Ryan replied, "but now I'm not so sure." He took a sip of punch.

"Oh, do you live here?" the boy asked, then added without waiting for the answer, "My name's Connor Walton."

Ryan nearly choked on the punch he was just then drinking. The only Connor Walton he knew was the two-year-old he had seen not very many minutes before, so it had to be somebody older who happened to have the same name, but hearing it unexpectedly had been a jolt. Unfortunately, in trying to recover from his surprise he half-pivoted on one foot and accidentally spilled some of his drink on the striped shirtfront of the beefy boy standing on the other side of him.

The beefy boy grabbed the front of Ryan's collar and pulled him in close.

"You splashed me!" he snarled in a gravelly voice that was unusually deep for a kid his age. Wherever he was from, he wasn't getting good dental care.

Meanwhile, Connor Walton sidled nervously away, wisely deciding that he didn't want to be part of *this* conversation.

"Er... sorry!" Ryan gulped. "I didn't mean to—"

"Why, I oughtta..." The boy pulled his free hand back as though he was about to send his fist sailing into Ryan's nose.

Then another boy stepped in, grabbing the beefy boy's wrist with a firm grip. "Hey, chill out, pal. This is a party."

The beefy boy looked blank. "Chill... what?"

"Yeah, chilling is good," Ryan added encouragingly.

The beefy boy scowled and lowered his hand as the other boy let go of it. "You fellows talk funny," he growled and turned away without another word.

Ryan managed a relieved smile. "Thanks for stepping in."

The other boy shrugged. Topped by a shaggy mop of light brown hair, he was fairly tall, lean and wiry, reminding Ryan by the way he moved of the boys he knew who played basketball. He also looked fairly normal in jeans and shirt, somehow like somebody Ryan knew, but as usual he couldn't place him.

14

"Hey, it's a party," the boy said. "It wouldn't be any fun if somebody slugged you."

"Not for me anyway," Ryan said. There was an awkward pause, and for lack of a better idea, he extended his hand. "I'm Ryan."

The other boy shook with him. "I'm Bill. Any idea what this is all about? I go down into my basement and suddenly this door that's been locked all my life opens up and here I am. Weird, huh?"

"Same thing happened to me," Ryan said, wondering how many houses in the world had basements with mysterious locked doors in them.

"And the heck of it is," Bill added, "half the kids here seemed kind of familiar, but when I took a closer look, I didn't know any of them at all."

"I've noticed the same thing," Ryan replied. "I even have a feeling I've seen you somewhere before."

"Maybe at school? You don't go to Centerpoint High, do you? I'm a sophomore there."

"I'm a sophomore there, too, but I don't think I've ever seen you around."

"Same here and I thought I knew everybody on sight."

Suddenly Ryan felt very cold. A terrible suspicion started to take shape in his mind. "Bill," he said slowly, "you said you came in through a door in your basement. What's your address?"

"128 West Fairground Street. Why?"

Ryan's mind raced. Trim and thin Bill's hair, age him a couple dozen years, put glasses on him, imagine him staring at a computer screen... He felt the room starting to spin.

"What's wrong?" Bill asked. "You're looking a little pale."

"We've got to talk. Privately." Ryan grabbed Bill's wrist and pulled him towards the open archway.

The adjoining room was unlit except for an open fireplace with a cheerfully crackling fire blazing away, and an enormous Christmas tree lavishly decorated with glistening ornaments and shining lights, with a multitude of brightly wrapped presents in piles underneath. Ryan guessed that all the kids at the party would shortly be ushered into this room, presents would be distributed, and then there would probably be games and maybe dancing for those who liked that sort of thing. For the moment, all that mattered was that nobody else was in the room just then.

"What is it?" Bill was starting to seem a little irritated. It wasn't obvious in his voice but there was something in his expression. Ryan knew the signs only too well. "There were some cookies I haven't tried yet."

"Look, er... Bill," Ryan began, not sure how to say what he didn't even want to admit to himself. "Did you see how half the kids in there are

15

dressed? It's like they're wearing historical costumes, except the old guy with the mustache told me it was a 'come as you are' party. Maybe he was trying to be mysterious, but now it's starting to make sense."

"So what?"

Ryan exhaled. It was time to drop the bomb. "If you're who I think you are, you're—"

"Hey, did they decide to move the party in here?" It was the girl in the red jumpsuit, coming in with a half-eaten cookie in one hand.

Bill glowered at her. "We were talking," he said coldly, making sure she understood that the people talking didn't include her.

"So?" she asked, unfazed as she joined them. "I can talk, too. What about?"

"None of your business!" Bill snapped.

"Then I'll make it my business!" Red Jumpsuit snapped back.

They were practically on the point of butting heads and baring their teeth. The intent expressions on their faces, their body language as they tensed for a confrontation, their posture... were nearly identical. *You'd think they were related*, Ryan said to himself, then the full implication of *that* idea hit him.

"Calm down, you two!" he urged, and turned to Bill. "Let her stay. I don't know how, but I have a feeling it *is* her business."

"Yes, but—" Bill started to say.

All of a sudden, an electric crackling exploded from the next room. Kids started yelling, some screaming. Startled, Ryan looked to see what was going on, but some kind of seething energy barrier blocked the archway, and it looked as though trying to pass through it would be a good way to be barbecued.

A loud voice, harsh and grating, cut through the noise. "Nobody move!"

"What's going—?" Red Jumpsuit started to say, but Bill shushed her with a finger to his lips.

He looked around, then pointed. At the back of the dimly lit room was a small alcove, almost invisible in the shadows. With a curt wave of his hand, Bill motioned for the other two to follow him.

The alcove probably served as a preparation area for buffets and banquets, with cupboards, a counter, even a sink. At the moment, it was the best place to hide.

"What's the idea?" the girl protested.

"Be quiet!" Bill whispered urgently. "I don't know what's going on in the other room but I think we'd better lie low until we figure it out. Now get down!"

As they hunkered in the shadows, the sounds of confusion and shuffling and the protests of unhappy kids continued from the adjoining room. Ryan could have sworn it was that beefy kid in the striped shirt he heard complaining, "I didn't get enough to eat yet!"

The energy curtain in the archway abruptly sizzled and snapped, then blinked out. A strangely short and bulky, even bow-legged man stepped into the room and quickly glanced around. He was wearing a black uniform that glistened like some combination of vinyl and rubber, and what looked like a chrome helmet. But his face — it looked more like a pig's snout than a nose. In the party room behind the trooper, Ryan could see other soldiers were not very gently lining the kids up in front of an open doorway in the far wall that hadn't been there before.

Ryan felt Bill and the girl both tense. All three held their breath.

After a long, long moment, the trooper turned and went back through the archway, and the energy barrier crackled into life again.

They let their breath out in a relieved sigh. It had been the quickest possible check of the room to see if any kids were in there. The man probably hadn't been expecting that there would be, didn't see any at a glance, and with his initial assumptions apparently confirmed, hadn't given the room a thorough inspection. Ryan suspected that if he really had wanted to give the room a serious lookover, they would have been found almost immediately.

"We just wanted to do something nice for the children!" they heard Uncle Gadwell exclaim from the other room, above the crackle of the energy curtain. "You have no right to do this!"

Someone snarled in reply, a voice that sounded more like jagged edges of metal rasping against each other than anything that would come out of a soft and moist throat, "Shut up and come with us."

That was followed by what was probably Mrs. Gadwell's voice, sounding worried and fearful. "What about the children?"

"Let the Master worry about them! Get moving!"

After a further minute or so of confusion, some shouting and complaining, and a lot of muttering and mumbling, things quieted down to silence. The energy curtain continued to crackle and sputter.

"Are they gone?" Ryan asked after nothing had been heard from the other room for a while.

"Sounds like it," Bill said, standing up.

"Was hiding a good idea?" the girl asked. "Maybe we should have turned ourselves in and they would have sent us home."

"That bunch?" Bill demanded. "Did they sound like they're the good guys? At least this way we got us some time to look around and figure things out."

17

"So where do we go?" The girl poked her wristband with her finger. "I can't get a sig on my com, so who knows where we even are?" She glanced at the energy curtain in the archway. "And we sure can't get back out that way."

Ryan started for the closed door in the opposite wall. "Maybe through there."

He had no idea where it led, but it was the only available route to anywhere. He opened the door and stepped through, and the other two followed.

They came out into a long, shadowy hallway lit by palely glowing spheres in the ceiling, with doors at intervals along both walls. By this time, they were well beyond the basement of Ryan's house. That hall would have stretched across the street and far beyond. It reminded him more of a hotel his family had once stayed at, though much larger, as the hallway seemed to be lost in some unlikely distance in both directions without any visible end.

After making sure the door wasn't locked on this side, in case they had to go back through it, Ryan closed it behind them. If those troopers returned, there was no point in making it obvious somebody had escaped this way.

For a moment, they stood there, looking up and down the hall, with no clear idea of what to do next.

"I guess we should introduce ourselves," the girl said when the indecision had been wearing on a little too long. "I'm Talitha."

Bill didn't seem to think getting chummy was exactly the most important item on the agenda just then, but went along with it. "My name's Bill."

"That's kind of an old-fashioned name," Talitha replied rather bluntly. "The only other person I know named Bill is my grandfather."

Why am I not surprised? Ryan thought with a clammy feeling. Knowing only too well what was coming next, he added, "And I'm Ryan."

Talitha blinked in surprise. "That's my dad's name. Funny coincidence, huh?"

No, it was anything but a coincidence. Ryan swallowed hard. While his suspicion had just been confirmed, her father's name was only half the story. The other half was something he shouldn't know, but he still had to ask.

"What's... your mother's name?"

During the pause as Talitha looked at him oddly, Ryan's mind raced to consider the possibilities. Lots of people, maybe even most people, didn't marry people they knew in school. It was perfectly possible he was destined to marry somebody he would meet in college or even later. It didn't have to be somebody he already knew. But if it was... April seemed

the most likely one. Yes. It would have to be April...
Then Talitha shrugged and said simply—
"Kelsey."

Chapter Three

Ryan's jaw dropped. Annoying, irritating Kelsey? But now that he looked at Talitha, especially those big green eyes, he saw the resemblance. It had been the boyishly short hair that had kept him from seeing it before. But it wasn't just Kelsey he saw in her. Talitha was a blend that included something else, and he could also see a resemblance between her and Bill. Who was *his* father. Which meant that the other element was... *himself.*

As he desperately tried to absorb the onslaught of too much information much too soon, he managed to blurt, "Did your father ever mention anybody named April?"

Talitha shook her head. "I don't think he has... but that's the name of one of my mother's old school friends. Mom's had her and her partner over at the house now and then."

"Her *partner*? You mean like her husband or boyfriend?"

"Neither one. April married another woman."

That probably explains why I didn't marry her, Ryan thought a little gloomily. Now he knew the April option had never been on the table at all.

"How about Caitlin?" he pressed. "Do you know anybody named Caitlin?"

"Where are you getting this stuff? That's the name of one of my mother's other friends. Only she marries men."

"You make it sound like it's happened more than once."

"Oh, lots of times. Mom says the next time Caitlin gets married, she's only sending an e-card because she can't afford to buy a present every time she turns around."

"Caitlin always was popular..." Ryan muttered.

"But it's really weird," Talitha went on cheerfully. "Dad knew Mom in school but he didn't even like her then because she was always pestering

20

him. Mom says she liked him from the moment they first met but didn't know how to tell him, and giving him the kazzle all the time was just her way of trying to get him to notice her."

"It must have worked..." Ryan said faintly, not even trying to figure out what a kazzle was and when he had gotten one. "How do they get along now?"

"Oh, just great. Dad says Mom isn't nearly as annoying now as she was back in school. I guess she grew out of it. In fact, he says he finally realized one day that he really did like her and those annoying little things she did were so much a part of her that they were why he got to like her."

The logic defied Ryan's understanding. He would probably have to be a lot older before he figured it out.

Bill had been listening to all this somewhere between complete incomprehension and utter boredom until his impatience got the better of him and he broke in. "I don't know what you two are talking about, but shouldn't we be thinking about how to get out of this mess?"

"First we have to figure out how big a mess we're in," Ryan said, "and I don't think either of you realize the half of it."

"What do you mean?" Talitha asked.

"How can I explain this..." Ryan looked at Bill. "Your name is Bill Thayer, and your father's name is Paul Thayer."

"How do you know all that?" Bill demanded, astonished.

"Because you're my father. Or will be."

"*What?*"

Talitha just rolled her eyes, then the dawn broke. "Wait a sec. All that stuff you knew, and you're Ryan Thayer? Are you saying you're my... my...?"

"Afraid so."

She looked at him again, suspiciously at first, then more closely — and she *knew*.

"Daddy...?" she gulped, her eyes suddenly wet.

"Ryan's fine," he said quickly, not sure if she was going to hug him or break down in tears or both at once. Fortunately, she held back, just staring at him with wide eyes and trembling a bit.

"But that's crazy," Bill insisted. "We're all the same age. How can...?"

"How should I know?" Ryan exclaimed. "Ask the old guy. I don't know how he worked it, but all those kids at the party were from different time periods. It wasn't just a Thayer family reunion, though. One of them was a neighbor kid from down the street. He was two when I saw him earlier today but he was about fourteen when I saw him just now."

"And that girl in the bonnet I was talking to…" Talitha said, her sentimental moment apparently over. "I didn't get much out of her that made any sense, but she did say her name was Thayer and her family had just started a farm here…"

Our great-great-grandmother? Ryan wondered.

Meanwhile, Bill had been puzzling it out, slowly and reluctantly accepting what was now only too obvious. "So if I'm your father, does that make this girl my granddaughter?"

Geeze, Dad, get a clue! "It's like that story about Scrooge. You know… I'm Christmas Present, you're Christmas Past, and she's Christmas Future."

"Why do I have to be the past?" Bill asked. "It sure feels like the present to me. No, I'm Christmas Present. You're Christmas Future and she's Christmas Future Future."

Talitha snorted. "And to me you're both guys who probably listened to President Lincoln on the radio. How about getting back to finding a way out of here?"

It's more like the Father, the Son, and the Holy Terror, Ryan thought. "Okay, maybe these doors lead somewhere."

He tried the next one down. Unlike the other doors, which were solid and blank, this one had a frosted glass window in it and opened onto a perfectly ordinary bathroom. That could be handy, but it wasn't what they needed just now.

He opened the following door and found himself looking out on a street scene in broad daylight on what seemed to be a warm spring day. Downtown in a small town in the 19th Century it looked like. A young man on a high-wheeled bicycle rode by and tipped his derby to Ryan as he went. As Ryan closed the door, he heard a crash that sounded ominously like a bicycle accident, as though the young man had been too distracted by tipping his hat to watch where he was going. Ryan opened the door again to see what had happened, but now there was only gray murk in front of him. Reclosing the door, he could only wonder if the wrecked bicycle his grandfather had reported seeing in the basement room had just been accounted for.

"Darnedest thing," Bill called from up the hall. "I opened this door and saw a log cabin, like it was a couple of hundred years ago and maybe where that Little House in the Cornfield girl was from, then everything turned to fog while I was looking at it."

What the heck…? Ryan suddenly had a bad feeling. "Quick, you two!" he exclaimed. "Get back in the room we came out of — *now!*"

Bill and Talitha both looked puzzled, but followed him into the room at a trot.

"What's the problem this time?" Talitha asked, irritated. "I was look-ing at a city with flying cars and—"

"That's the problem," Ryan said, and pointed out the doorway. The corridor was gone, replaced by swirling gray fog. "I guess the hallway's some kind of tunnel through time, and all those doors lead to different periods in the past and future. But when the doorways started going gray, I realized they don't stay open very long once they're opened. If we'd waited a few more seconds, we probably couldn't have gotten back in here and we'd be stuck out in the hall with nowhere to go."

"And this place is any better?" Bill asked.

"Well, it is the only place we've seen with any connection to home," Ryan replied.

"Look!" Talitha gestured to the archway leading to the party room. The wall of energy in the archway was gone, but the room beyond was now dark. "Maybe we can go back that way."

"We can try," Ryan said, trying to sound more confident than he felt.

Talitha stepped boldly to the threshold. Ryan wanted to call her back in case something dangerous they hadn't noticed yet was waiting in the darkness beyond, but instead of going on in, she touched her left index finger to something on the band on her right wrist. Whatever else it was or did, it had a built-in flashlight. A concentrated beam of light shot out and she adjusted its spread more widely. Then she gasped.

Now Ryan and Bill had joined her, and they saw why she had given a start. It wasn't just that the lights had been turned out in the party room. The party room was gone. Instead, there was just a dusty room with spider-webs and random junk, including an ancient bicycle with an enormous bent front wheel leaning against one wall. Along another wall was some metal shelving with dusty glass beakers and test-tubes, and over in the far corner was a heavy wooden table with only three legs. It was the mys-terious room as it had been described to Ryan and as he had always assumed it would look. No decorations, no food, no people. Broken glass-ware crunched underfoot on the concrete floor as they stepped inside to look around. Behind them, the room with the Christmas tree vanished into gray fog, then the archway closed up into a solid wall matching the dirty concrete blocks around it.

"At least now we know where we are," Bill said.

"But *when* are we?" Ryan asked.

"It's sure not my time," Talitha declared. "This room was all cleaned up by then and made into a rec room. That's how I got here. I came down to watch some vids and took some kind of wrong turn and then I was at that party."

Ryan went to the door that led out into the rest of the basement and tried the knob. It turned and the door opened. Outside was the basement as he remembered it, dusty with a few dim overhead light bulbs still on. It could be his time, or it could be Bill's. The broken baby carriage would look about the same in either case.

"Maybe if we walk through the doorway one at a time," he said hopefully, "it'll send us back to where each of us came from."

"We might as well try it," Bill said not so hopefully. "It's the only direction we can go."

Ryan stepped through the doorway first. It was definitely the same basement he had left, with the same jelly jars on the shelves. Unfortunately... Bill and Talitha came through the doorway right behind him. It had sent them back to where the doorway had last been set. To Ryan's time. Now all three were in the basement together.

Talitha looked disgustedly around the dingy basement. "Got any more bright ideas, *Dad?*"

Chapter Four

Almost absently, Bill closed the door behind him. It clicked loudly. Realizing his possible mistake, he turned and tried to open it again. The lock might as well have been rusted solid and the knob refused to turn. "Oops..." The door was now as Ryan remembered it, old and battered with peeling paint, and without a wreath in sight.

"Not a problem," Ryan said. "If you left it open, who knows what might come through after us?" He thought of the trooper with the pig snout.

"Are we going to stay down here or what?" Talitha asked. "It's kinda dirty."

Ryan was forced to admit to himself that he had completely run out of ideas, bright or otherwise. All he could do now was take them upstairs and hope the adults could think of something. For that matter... maybe his father would know what to do. That was his younger self right there, after all, and surely he would remember what had happened and how they got out of this.

"Come on," Ryan said, leading them up the basement steps. "It's time to meet the family." *Boy, is this going to take some explaining...*

Mrs. Thayer was working at the kitchen sink, and looked up as Ryan came through the basement doorway.

"Did you bring the raspberry jelly—" she started to ask, then saw Bill and Talitha come after him. "Oh, I didn't know you had friends over. I didn't see them...?" She trailed off as she got a good look at Bill, and her hand flew to her mouth to stifle a shriek.

Ryan's mother and father had met in college, when William Thayer was still young enough that he wouldn't have looked much different from his teenage self.

Bill returned the stare, just as astonished. Well, of course. This was his future wife, a woman he hadn't even met yet and already nearly forty years old. That had to take some getting used to.

Talitha was also looking a little oddly at Mrs. Thayer. "Grandma...?" she whispered, recognizing her even though the woman she knew by that title was considerably older.

Mrs. Thayer dropped her hand long enough to shout, "BILL!" Ryan couldn't tell whether it was a shocked cry of recognition or a frantic call for her husband.

William Thayer the Elder had still been working at his computer in the parlor, and came running when he heard the yell. He stopped short in the kitchen, suddenly confronted with Bill the Younger.

For a long moment, the two stared at each other. Seeing them together, they were obviously and undeniably the same person at different stages of life. One was a little shorter than the other and they were a quarter of a century apart, but probably neither was familiar enough with what he looked like from the outside to quite grasp what everyone else could plainly see.

Yet neither was all that surprised. Bill would have been expecting to find his older self upstairs, and Mr. Thayer muttered, "I'm starting to remember something... I was supposed to forget, but there was something about this..."

How he could have forgotten in the first place was beyond Ryan, unless there had been some deliberate tampering with his memory by someone to make sure he forgot. That ominous thought made him realize this adventure wasn't over by a long shot.

Some amount of explanation followed, interspersed with Mrs. Thayer at first refusing to believe any of it, but the evidence was right in front of her. Not just her husband of the past but her granddaughter of the future, and in the end she had to accept it.

On the other hand, Mr. Thayer took it surprisingly well. In fact, he even seemed to be enjoying the situation more than he really should have.

"Look at me!" he exclaimed to his wife, referring to his younger self. "I look like my Senior Picture!"

Then Grandma appeared in the doorway. Sometimes she liked to go to her bedroom and take a nap in the late afternoon before coming down to help with dinner.

"What's all the commotion?" she started to ask, and Young Bill saw her.

"Mom—?" he choked, recognizing the short and rather round old woman with gray hair as his mother a quarter of a century after he had last seen her, an hour or two earlier.

And she recognized her son as he had been a quarter of a century before. "Billy?" She didn't faint, but she looked as though she would have liked to, just to gain some time to absorb what she was seeing.

Now Grandma had to be brought on board as well, which took a few more minutes to straighten out. She had never seen Talitha before in any shape or form, and that meant some additional explaining.

"Then you're my great-granddaughter?" Grandma said with a quaver in her voice.

Talitha nodded. "And you're my great-grandmother. I've seen you in pics."

It may have not been the most tactful thing to say, making it only too clear that they would never meet again, but Grandma just smiled and hugged her, accepting the miracle for what it was without inquiring about the details. "I don't know how you got here, but I'm glad you came."

Something completely impossible may have just happened, but dinner still had to be prepared. After the initial shock and disbelief had faded a little, Mrs. Thayer suggested that Ryan show Bill and Talitha around the house. It seemed a little unnecessary since both had grown up in it, if at different times, and knew it as well as he did, but he caught a glance from his father that seemed to say, "Grown-ups need to talk."

As tours went, it was a quick one, with Bill mainly remarking on how little had changed in the house since his time. That made sense since his parents still lived in it.

For Talitha's part, she said, "It's like looking at an old photo. Sometimes you wonder what it would be like if you could go inside the picture and look around. I think now I know."

When they glanced into the living room, Bill saw Grandpa still dozing in his chair and muttered, "Dad…?"

Talitha saw Ryan's little sister, still watching cartoons on TV, and murmured, "Aunt Jessie…?"

Back in the hall, Bill wondered out loud, "Didn't Mom and Dad ever get new furniture? That's the same couch and recliner!"

Talitha just complained, "That vidscreen is really ancient! It's not even 3-D!"

"What's to gripe about?" Bill demanded. "I would have loved to have a screen that big. It's like being at the movies!"

"What's so great about being at the movies?" Talitha shot back. "We can be *in* the movies if we want!"

Bill looked briefly puzzled and Ryan was about to explain that she probably meant movies in her time were interactive, but then he wondered if he would have to explain to him what "interactive" meant.

Meanwhile, Bill's mind had moved on to something else. Now he wanted to see his old room on the second floor, so they went upstairs. The room currently belonged to Ryan's little brother and of course was furnished differently than it had been when Bill lived in it.

"What, your brother has his own TV set?" Bill exclaimed. "I didn't have one when I was that age! What are all those little cases? Videotapes of movies?"

Ryan shook his head. "Tapes are pretty much dead now. Those are videogames."

"Really? Looks like games have come a long way since Donkey Kong and Pac-Man. D'you think he'd get mad if I played one?"

Dad! Keep your mind on business! "Er... later, maybe."

The room that would someday be Talitha's was currently occupied by Ryan's little sister, but looking at it didn't seem to tell Talitha anything she didn't already know, other than that her aunt's love for stuffed animals of all sorts had started very young.

From there it was up the narrow steps to the attic. Two rooms had been finished into bedrooms, though only Ryan's was being used at the moment, while the other half was still plain attic. Like the basement, it was filled with the accumulated clutter of generations. Since the attic environment was more benign, if a bit dusty, this was where unused items went that somebody might still want someday, while more obvious junk was consigned to the oblivion of the basement. Just glancing around, Ryan saw stacks of boxes, some round as though for hats, an old-fashioned dress form, a crank-operated phonograph with a huge speaker horn, a laserdisc player that had been the leading edge of technology and in active use downstairs just hours before by Bill's personal clock, and a steamer trunk with faded but still colorful stickers showing that someone had made a thorough job of seeing the world probably well before World War II.

"All this stuff's still here?" Bill exclaimed. "Most of it hasn't moved since my time!"

"So this is what the attic looked like before they remodeled it," Talitha said without much interest. "Looks like a garage sale waiting to happen." As she spoke, she glanced absently at her wristband. Not for the first time, Ryan realized.

"What are you doing?" Bill asked. "You keep looking at that thing like you expect it to do something."

Talitha dropped her hand to her side, a little embarrassed that she had been noticed. "I kind of am. Force of habit. You don't know what being off the beam is like. It's never happened to me before and it's scary. Nobody knows where I am, nobody can find me, I can't call anybody or even get a sig... I'm completely cut off from everything."

Bill shrugged. "So welcome to my world, kid."

"Actually, it's mine," Ryan said, "but I think I know what she means.

What she's talking about has already started. I just read a manga where the writer wanted to get a girl lost on a class field trip and she had to lose her cell phone first so she couldn't just call for help."

"A what-ga?"

"Oh, a Japanese comic. After your time."

"I've heard of comics," Talitha said, brightening. "They were kind of like movies on paper, only they didn't move, right?"

Talitha's use of the past tense for comics didn't escape Ryan's notice, and it was a little sad to find out they would go the way of silent movies.

"Something like that," he agreed, mainly to keep from dwelling on it, and proceeded to show them his own room.

That went quickly since there wasn't much to see beyond the standard bed, dresser, and small desk. Bill and Talitha were more interested in the TV set, the DVD player, and the few movies and books.

Talitha picked up a DVD at random and looked at it puzzledly. "Oh, I see!" she exclaimed after a moment. "The vid's in here when it isn't playing!"

"Where else would it be?" Ryan had to ask.

"In a membloc somewhere, of course. All we have to do is get on the beam and we can down any vids we want. Books, too. Having to store all your vids and books in your house even when you're not looking at them must waste a lot of space."

"I don't exactly have enough for it to be a problem," Ryan admitted. *I could tell her about iPods and e-books and streaming since her world's practically halfway here now, but they'd probably seem old-fashioned to her, too...*

She picked up one of the textbooks he had dropped earlier on his bed and looked at it, at first apparently not quite certain which end it opened from. "You're studying French? Why bother?"

"Er... Does France get wiped out or something?"

"No, just that nobody has to speak foreign languages any more. We have things we can put in our ears that translate everything into English if we need it. And if you're really serious about learning a language, you can get a memmod implanted. It costs, though."

"Sounds great," Ryan said, "but the world I live in isn't quite there yet and I need to take a foreign language so I can get into college and get a good job so I can support you when you come along. Is that enough reason?"

She stuck her tongue out at him and turned away to check out his other textbooks.

Ryan had a sudden thought. "Wait a minute... how is it that you grew up in this house, too? What kind of job did I get? Didn't I ever get out of this town?"

Talitha looked back at him and was about to say something, then had a sudden thought of her own and started over. "I could tell you, but I don't want to murph it. Let's just say you figured something out."

It would help if I knew what I figured out... but it didn't look as though nagging Talitha to tell him anyway would do any good.

Bill was amazed to see that like his brother, Ryan also had a TV set of his own, "I sure am spoiling you kids!"

The TV had been a hand-me-down in more prosperous times a couple of years before when Ryan's parents got a new one, but no need to go into detail. *What I really need is my own computer since you're on the one downstairs all the time...* With the current state of family finances, however, that didn't seem like something that would happen very soon.

What Bill didn't see was what really caught his attention. "No baseball bat... no glove... no basketball...?"

"I guess I'm just not really into sports," Ryan admitted.

Bill's eyebrows went up. "And you're supposed to be my son? Are you sure you weren't adopted?"

Fortunately, Ryan knew Bill's older version well enough to sense from his voice and body language when he was kidding. At least he hoped he was, but since Ryan's lack of interest in anything to do with kicking, hitting, or throwing balls of various sizes and configurations had always been a minor irritant between him and his father, it did sting a bit.

Bill went to the window and looked out at the sky and treetops. "I wouldn't mind having this room," he said a little dreamily, "but there aren't as many people living in the house in my time and this is one of the rooms that aren't being used. Oh well, it's a little too far from the bathroom anyway."

When they came back downstairs, it was to discover that the grown-ups' conference about the crisis hadn't led to any firm conclusions after all. Mr. Thayer had tried to remember what had happened (and was currently happening to his younger self), but he hadn't come up with anything more specific than some vague impressions and half-remembered fragments of dreams that he couldn't quite piece together. It was enough to know that what was happening was real and serious, however, and he had been able to convince his wife and mother of at least that much.

By this time, dinner was ready. "You can eat with us," Mrs. Thayer said to Bill and Talitha. "I set a couple of extra places."

Talitha moaned. "Oh no! I shouldn't have eaten all those cookies..."

There was a sound stirring from the living room. "Eat? Did somebody say it was time to eat? I'm coming."

A rustle followed as Grandpa put his newspaper down and got up from his chair. Ryan was a little surprised to realize that Grandpa had dozed through all the uproar of the cross-time family reunion in the kitchen, but the merest mention of dinner had roused him.

Grandpa came into the dining room, and it struck Ryan that he looked like a thin version of Uncle Gadwell, a lean old man with white hair and a full white mustache.

Grandpa saw Bill and blinked. He looked at Mr. Thayer, then at Bill again. Then he saw Talitha and sighed. "So it's finally happened. I was afraid of this."

Explanations in varying degrees of complexity had to be made to Ryan's brother and sister to account for the unexpected guests, but neither was really old enough to understand the full story and much of the ensuing conversation at dinner went right by them.

"Just look at those two!" Mrs. Thayer marveled to her husband, referring to Ryan and Talitha sitting next to each other across the big dining-room table from her. "You'd think they were brother and sister! I wonder who her mother is?"

"You've met her," Ryan said. "Remember back in October when I was doing that class project and I had some kids over one night to work on it?"

"You mean that tall girl with the short hair?" Mrs. Thayer asked. "I thought she had her eye on you but I didn't want to say anything about it at the time."

Mom already figured it out? How come I'm always the last to know about these things?

Sensing Ryan's discomfort with the subject, Mr. Thayer turned to his own father at the head of the table. "So you knew all about this, Dad?"

Grandpa nodded. "Enough to be half-expecting it, anyway. Pass the butter, somebody? I'd prefer to wait until after dinner to tell you what I know, though. It's a little complicated."

Mrs. Thayer smiled benevolently at Talitha. "Eat all you like, dear. It must be nice to eat solid food for a change."

Talitha looked blank. "Solid food... huh?"

"You're from the future, aren't you?" Mrs. Thayer said in all innocence. "Don't you live on pills instead of eating?"

"We eat food, same as you do!" Talitha protested.

Ryan nudged her. "Mom's just kidding." *At least I hope she is.* She didn't seem to be laughing, though...

Bill turned to his older self. "Did you ever manage to find a Hank Aaron rookie card?"

31

"Nope," Mr. Thayer replied sadly. "They were out there, but it would have taken three summers of mowing lawns to afford one. So I gave up."

Bill's face fell. "I knew it was a long shot, but I always hoped..."

"What are they talking about?" Talitha asked Ryan.

"Baseball cards, I think."

Talitha shook her head, not showing any sign that she even knew what such things were.

Mr. Thayer changed the subject to something more cheerful. "If they've cleared the snow off the blacktop, maybe we can run over to the grade school and shoot a few hoops."

"You're on," Bill grinned. "I bet I can whip your butt, old man!"

"Oh yeah? Don't be so sure, junior. You may be younger than me, but that just means I know a few things you haven't learned yet."

As things turned out, there wasn't any time for a pickup game. After dinner, everyone gathered in the living room. The adults took the chairs and the couch while the younger set found space on the floor.

Grandpa sat back in his easy chair, pressed his fingertips together in front of his chest, and cleared his throat. "I guess the place to start is that room downstairs that's been locked all these years. Old Uncle Gadwell didn't just have a chemistry set-up down there like everybody thought. He was really experimenting with something else. Magic, to be precise."

A pause followed while he let everyone digest that revelation.

"Oh, come on," Ryan blurted. "Magic isn't real!"

"Maybe not," Grandpa replied evenly, "but isn't that your daughter from the future sitting next to you?"

"Yeah, but—" Ryan started to say, then remembered all the science fiction he had read. "No, what I meant was that there has to be a scientific explanation. Maybe it isn't really magic but just super-advanced science. I remember reading about some science-fiction writer named Clarke who said—"

"That could be," Grandpa interrupted, probably wanting to spare everyone a time-consuming even if interesting discussion about the philosophy of science, "but Gadwell seemed to think it was magic. He got his start when a circus came to town and he was fascinated by a magician with the show who called himself Karlo the Magnificent. Most, well, pretty much all, magicians are simply performers doing conjuring tricks, of course, but Karlo was that rare exception who really did have magical powers. While traveling with the circus was a way to make a living, he was getting on in years and his real purpose was to find a successor, some-one with the potential and aptitude to carry on his work, and he thought such a person would likely be attracted to a show like his. Eventually he found Gadwell Thayer.

"After that, the details have been lost to time. All we really know is that Gadwell did something down in that room during his apprenticeship. Nobody in the family has ever been certain exactly what, but no one has been too anxious to look closely enough to find out, either. There's even a family legend that says he went into that room one day and never came back out. I don't know if it's true, but it would explain why I never knew him even though he should have still been around as an old man when I was a boy. That's why the door's been locked all these years. Some things are best left undisturbed. Judging from what you've said, my guess is that he found some way to open a door into time and other dimensions."

"All that power and he used it to have a Christmas party for a bunch of kids," Mr. Thayer said, shaking his head.

"Not the worst use of power I've ever heard of," Grandpa remarked. "The fact remains that despite his good intentions, somebody crashed the party and kidnapped him and all those kids. This is serious, and something needs to be done, both to rescue the victims and to send these two back to their own times—" He gestured to Bill and Talitha.

"We must have gotten back home," Bill said. "My grown-up self is right here, and so are my son and granddaughter. They're proof I got home all right. And Ryan's already home."

Talitha glared at Bill. "Where's the proof *I'll* get home?"

"I don't think we can just sit here and wait for the problem to solve itself," Grandpa went on. "Predestined or not, somebody has to *act* to make things happen. Besides, sending Bill and Talitha home isn't the only problem. The abducted children have to be returned to their own times, as well. Those children undoubtedly include some of our direct ancestors, after all. If anything happens to them, the consequences would be drastic for everyone in this room."

Talitha sighed. "It sounds pretty hopeless. What can we do?"

"We're all way out of our depth here," Grandpa said, "but I think we can get someone who knows what he's doing to help us."

"Who?" Mrs. Thayer asked. "Is there somebody we can report this to?"

"Not exactly," Grandpa told her. "Normally I'd say Gadwell is the logical person to straighten this mess out since he caused it, but now that he's been captured by powers unknown, he's out of the question. No, the only one who might be able to help us would be Karlo the Magnificent."

Ryan immediately thought of one obvious problem. "Uh... wouldn't he have died like about a hundred years ago?"

"Something like that," Grandpa said, "but that just means we'll have to catch him before his passing."

Everyone in the room looked startled, with a chorus of, "Huh? How?"

Grandpa quieted the outburst with a wave of his hand. "As it happens, this situation was not unforeseen. Just before he died, my father gave me a sealed envelope that Karlo had prepared, with instructions to open it in case of some mix-up in time due to Gadwell's meddling. I think the crisis we now face was known several generations back, and provisions were made even though it would be many years before they were necessary. It's just my luck that it finally happened in my lifetime and I couldn't pass the envelope on to Billy and let him worry about it."

"I never heard about any of this before," Mr. Thayer said in amazement, ignoring for the moment that his younger self was right there with him and hearing about it at the same time he was. "So where's the envelope?"

Grandpa rubbed his white stubbly chin. "Hmm... I'll have to think about that. I know I put it somewhere for safekeeping... Up in the attic, if I remember right."

Ryan thought of the attic and trying to find something put away fifty or more years ago in those stacks of boxes. Grandpa might still be looking for it next Christmas.

Mr. Thayer was apparently thinking the same thing. "This could take a while," he said. "There's a Christmas parade downtown tonight, so why don't you kids go watch it while Dad's trying to find the envelope? You can see how we do things in our time."

Since they couldn't do anything until the envelope turned up, it was as good an idea as any. With that, the meeting broke up.

While Grandpa headed for the attic, the others gathered in the front hall.

"It's a little cold out," Mrs. Thayer said. "Since you didn't bring your coat, Talitha, you can borrow one of mine."

"Er, thanks," Talitha replied, "but I don't need it." She patted her white belt. "Built-in heating unit."

"Oh, like wearing an electric blanket." Mrs. Thayer seemed suitably impressed, but added, "You'd better wear a coat anyway if you don't want people wondering how you can run around without one when it's freezing out there."

She found a parka for Talitha. The hood had the advantage of hiding her startling, nearly bald head, while the faux fur trim outlining her face gave the impression of hair behind it. Now she fit the local preconceptions of what a girl should look like, and hopefully wouldn't attract too much unwanted attention. Her tight shimmery red slacks and white boots weren't exactly the latest fashion trend, but they weren't entirely off the mark, either.

Ryan only had one winter coat, so Bill couldn't borrow any extras from him, but Mr. Thayer provided one of his own.

As Bill put the coat on, he noticed his fingers didn't extend very far out of his sleeves. "It's a little big for me..."

"Don't worry," Mr. Thayer said cheerfully. "You'll grow into it."

Chapter Five

The night was cold and clear with stars glittering overhead in an inky black sky. The brisk walk along the cleared sidewalks several blocks to downtown was almost pleasant.

Bill was surprised to see the brightly lit convenience store and gas station with a large parking lot at the corner of Fairground and Main.

"What happened to the MacEvoy house?" he asked.

Ryan had to think. "Burned down, I guess. We weren't living in Centerpoint then, and all I remember is that it was gone when we visited one summer when I was about five or six."

"Aw," Bill said with obvious disappointment, "I always wanted to live there when I grew up. Our house was okay, but that old place had turrets!"

"And it probably didn't have strange secret rooms in its basement, either," Ryan added.

"Another point in its favor," Bill said, and no one seemed inclined to disagree.

That led to a conversation as they walked up Main Street about how things had changed over time, but Ryan's attempt to explain current affairs was mostly lost on Bill. He would have preferred to hear who had won the World Series and the Superbowl every year for the last twenty-five years, while Ryan couldn't have told him the names of last year's winners.

On the other hand, Ryan was curious to hear about the world of his future, but asking Talitha about it didn't get him very far. The world she lived in was on the other side of some major upheavals over the next thirty years that she wasn't able to explain very well, but it was all perfectly normal to her and it was Ryan's problem if he couldn't understand the simplest little thing. Before he could narrow it down to more specific questions that might have straightforward answers, such as whether anybody had been to Mars yet, they had reached the first stores of downtown.

Main Street was brightly lit and decorated for the season, and crowds had already begun to collect along the sidewalks for the parade. They found a place to stand on the curb by a lamp pole, and glancing up, Bill saw a large plastic toy-soldier decoration hanging from it.

"I think that's the same Nutcracker the city had twenty-five years ago!" He looked around the street and added, "Looks like the old town hasn't changed much. Different names on the stores, cars look funny, a lot more vans on the street... that's about it." He noticed Talitha, was staring across the street as though she was seeing something that shouldn't be there. "I suppose it's really changed by your time?"

"Pretty much," she agreed. "They made downtown into a mall. All those buildings over there are gone and there's a park, and the street was closed to traffic."

Ryan suddenly had a queasy feeling of the seemingly solid buildings around him looking a little fuzzy at the edges. Of course things would be different in thirty years, but hearing it described by someone who had been there and had seen it was disconcerting. It didn't seem to bother Bill, though, who just then noticed something else.

They were standing in front of the movie theater, dark with letters on the marquee spelling out **CLOSED FOR REMODELING**, and Bill couldn't resist making the obvious joke.

"That's a funny name for a movie."

"Yeah," Ryan replied, his moment of disorientation passing, "but it's been showing for the last four or five years. Now we have to go to the multiplex out at the mall."

"Not surprised," Bill said. "Downtown was already dying in my time."

Then they watched the parade go by. Whether it had been worth the trip, Ryan wasn't sure. He mainly realized that he'd had some excellent reasons for wanting to skip the affair entirely. The parade wasn't much more than the high school marching band playing a more or less recognizable rendition of "Jingle Bells," some cars filled with local notables waving out the windows, and a few somewhat worn-looking floats maintained by local organizations that he remembered from the Fourth of July parade. Neither Bill nor Talitha seemed terribly interested, either, Bill because it wasn't any different from parades in his time, Talitha probably because it was just some quaint native festival of a bygone age to her.

"What are those little doodads people are holding up?" Bill asked.

Ryan looked and saw people along the sidewalk holding small devices in their upraised hands and pointing them at the parade.

"Their phones," he replied.

"They're holding their phones up?" Bill echoed in near-disbelief. "Why? So their friends back home can hear the music? It isn't that good."

"Actually," Ryan said, "they're taking pictures. Their phones have built-in cameras."

"Phones with cameras? Who came up with that idea? Do they have toasters, too?"

Talitha yawned. "Old stuff."

"In fact," Bill added for good measure, shooting a sideways grin at Ryan, "it's about as dumb an idea as a flashlight built into your sleeve!"

It took Talitha a second to realize she was being ribbed. "Hey! It comes in real handy now and then!"

The rear was brought up by a float that was a simulated housetop with Santa Claus stuffed to his waist in the faux chimney and waving to the crowd. In an earlier era, even before Bill's time, it might have been meant to signal the beginning of the Christmas season, but these days that actually started at midnight on October 31, when the drugstore cleared the Halloween candy off the shelves and put out the Christmas merchandise and decorations. Now the theory was that the parade celebrated the beginning of the local schools' winter vacation and the word "Christmas" wasn't even officially mentioned for some strange legal reason that no one wanted to talk about, not that calling it "Winterfest" really fooled anybody.

After the parade, the crowd dispersed. As cold as it was, there probably wasn't any reason to hang around, but Bill and Talitha seemed fascinated by looking at the displays in the brightly lit store windows.

"Where's the video store?" Bill asked. "I want to see what kind of movies are out now."

"The video store died years ago," Ryan had to tell him, "but we do have this." He indicated a red vending machine outside the drugstore.

"Huh," said Bill, and went over to take a look at what was available.

For Talitha, the latest videos might have been something like silent movies, old and forgotten and no more than dusty relics left behind by the march of technology, and her attention wandered to the window displays. The drugstore was the nearest thing to the long-gone Main Street department stores in the variety of merchandise it sold, and it especially stood out with a big window showing an assortment of current toys in a Christmassy, under-the-tree setting, though the big stores in the mall at the edge of town had a much better selection.

Talitha thought they were insufferably primitive. "I had a doll you could talk to," she declared, "and she'd answer you!"

Bill raised an eyebrow. "Had? What happened to it?"

"We had to give her away," Talitha said regretfully. "She wasn't getting along with the cat."

Before Ryan could inquire further, she saw a window display in the still-open candy store and doughnut bakery that even she couldn't scoff at.

"Buy me something, Daddy!" she exclaimed in a mock little girl's voice, grabbing his arm.

Ryan winced. "Don't push it, kid."

Suddenly, behind him, he heard an all too familiar voice. "I thought you weren't coming to the parade."

I should have known this would happen. Ryan turned around and saw Kelsey standing there, glaring at him and looking twice as menacing in her bulky winter coat. Just behind her were April and Caitlin, turned towards the street and rather pointedly staying out of this by pretending to be interested in watching the parade that had already gone by. Ryan had another queasy moment realizing that he knew more than he should about what the future would be for both of them.

Kelsey saw Ryan standing next to Talitha. And noticed Talitha holding on to Ryan's arm.

"So that's how it is," Kelsey said in a voice that sounded like icicles freezing. "You said you weren't going to the parade, but you were really going with *her*."

Oh Lord, Ryan thought wearily. *I'm actually beginning to understand her.* "I really didn't know I was going to be here," he said quickly, "but they wanted to see the parade." He gestured to Bill and Talitha. "Family. Visiting." *And it's even true!*

"Oh..." Kelsey still wasn't very happy but she was starting to waver and probably wondering if it was worth staying mad. "Your cousins?"

"Something like that."

He was suddenly aware of Talitha next to him. She was unconsciously squeezing his arm a little too tightly, and he heard her gulp, a strangled sob. He glanced at her. She was staring at Kelsey.

And Kelsey was staring at her. "You two do look a lot alike," she said slowly, "but there's something else..."

Something else? Seeing them together, their resemblance was jaw-droppingly obvious, beginning with the big green eyes and working down. If this had been a movie, Talitha and Kelsey would have been played by the same actress using split-screen.

Talitha couldn't hold back any longer. Before Ryan could stop her, she bolted forward and threw herself at Kelsey.

Kelsey staggered back a step as Talitha hugged her, crying and sobbing. "Hey!" Kelsey yelped. "Get this crazy chick off me! Is your whole family nuts?"

No, Ryan wanted to say, *she probably gets it from* your *side.*

Bill stepped next to Ryan and asked in a low voice. "What's going on?"

"We just ran into her mother."

Bill whistled. "Whew. Sticky situation. At least your future wife is the same age you are. Mine's like about forty and I still don't know how to deal with that. Can't complain about your taste, though, son."

"You don't know her, Pappy." Ryan went to pull Talitha off Kelsey, murmuring into her ear, "Take it easy, kid. There'll be plenty of time for hugging Mommy later." *A lot later*, he added to himself. While Talitha got her self-control back and Kelsey smoothed down the front of her long coat with a highly displeased look on her face, Ryan decided to make a hasty introduction that would plausibly explain everything, then proceed to a quick getaway. "This is Bill," he told Kelsey, "and this is Talitha."

Kelsey stared. "Talitha...? That's funny."

"What's so funny about my name?" Talitha wondered. "You're the one who—"

Ryan jabbed her with his elbow. "Not now!"

"I don't mean funny ha-ha," Kelsey said slowly. "I mean it's funny because..." She turned to Ryan. "How can your cousin be named that? It's not even a common name! It's something I saw somewhere when I was little, and... well, I thought it might be a cool name for a princess in a story I was writing, and ever since I even had the idea I might name my daughter that, if I ever have one, and of course if my husband goes along with it..." She trailed off.

Uh oh... She's about ten seconds away from figuring it out. And things will get really complicated if she does.

"Just one of those things," he said brightly. "Coincidences are weird that way. Well, see you in school next year! Merry Christmas!" He grabbed Talitha's arm. "Come on, let's go!"

"Merry Christmas... I guess," Kelsey replied a little faintly, probably realizing that something important had just happened and she had no idea what.

They left Kelsey to untangle the inexplicable on her own and went down the block to look in other store windows. On the way, Talitha giggled to herself.

"Now what?" Ryan asked.

"So that was Mom as a girl! It was almost worth the trip just to see that!" Then her tone abruptly turned serious. "Da— er, Ryan, Great-Grandpa will find a way to send me home, won't he? I don't think I can take much more of this."

Ryan had to admit that running into relatives thirty years younger than they should have been probably was a little straining emotionally. He was feeling some of it himself with just these two.

"Don't worry," he said, trying to pass it off lightly. "Even if you are stuck here, we can always say you're my orphaned cousin and we adopted you. Now isn't such a bad time to live in."

Ryan could see the horror on Talitha's face even in the semi-darkness as she reacted to that idea. "Oh God," she murmured to herself, "just kill me now and get it over with..."

Ryan's phone beeped. He pulled it out of his pocket, saw from the display that someone was calling from the house, and put it to his ear.

His father (the one at home, not the one next to him) was on the other end. "You kids had better come on back, Ryan. Your grandfather just found the envelope."

Chapter Six

When they got home (and it was home for all three of them, if not concurrently), Mr. Thayer met them at the door and led them into the dining room. There, Grandpa sat at the now cleared table, holding a purplish, ancient-looking envelope a little larger than the usual 9x12 and bulging from something small but lumpy inside.

As they came in, he spilled the contents onto the table. Money mostly, but three rings also fell out, shining silver with strange symbols engraved on the outer edges.

"Put these on," Grandpa said, handing them out to Ryan and the others. "You need to talk to Karlo, and these magic rings are set to send you back to a day in July, 1895 when the circus he was traveling with was in town."

He said it as casually as though he was sending them out for a walk around the block. All three goggled in stunned silence.

"Do I have to go?" Ryan finally asked. "I'm already home."

In reply, Grandpa held up a yellowed sheet of paper with a swirling mass of florid calligraphy inked on it. "According to the notes Karlo left, the rings only work together, so all three of you do in fact have to go. Sorry, Ryan. You were at that party and time is out of joint for you as well. I can't say I like sending fifteen-year-olds out on a job like this, but Karlo's notes are clear on the point that only the three of you can straighten things out. Even so, I had a dickens of a time while you were at the parade convincing your mother to let you go. Your father had to talk her into it, but then he already went and came back. He's more convinced that history can't be changed than I am, so don't get too confident out there."

A job like this? Just the sound of it made Ryan feel uneasy. What kind of job?

"Just when I thought things couldn't get any weirder..." Talitha muttered.

"When I was your age, I would have loved to travel through time," Grandpa said with rather forced good cheer. "Look at it as an adventure."

"Yeah, but isn't it starting to feel like maybe a little too much for one day?" Bill asked.

Grandpa ignored the question and turned to the money that had been in the envelope. "You'll need this to get into the circus, and trying to use modern money would just get you arrested for counterfeiting."

He passed the money out, amounting to two two-dollar bills and a single silver dollar along with some small change for each of them.

Ryan noticed that the two-dollar bills were larger than modern banknotes while the coins were the familiar sizes but had unfamiliar designs. "Will this be enough?"

"Probably," Grandpa said. "You shouldn't be there that long. Remember, money went a lot further in those days than it does now, so you've actually got a tidy little fortune there. Just don't go crazy spending it."

"What about clothes?" Bill wondered. "Weren't they kind of different way back when?"

"We don't have time to outfit you kids with 1890s duds," Grandpa replied, "but you boys should be fine. Shirts and pants haven't changed a whole lot, and you're young enough you can get by without wearing hats. Talitha, though..." He appraised her shiny red jumpsuit. "Just get in and out as fast as you can. With her short hair, people will probably think she's a boy at first glance anyway."

Talitha winced. "Thanks a lot."

"So how do we find Karlo?" Ryan asked.

"That's actually the easy part." Grandpa sounded as though he was glad that he finally had something positive to report. "The street outside wasn't named Fairground Street for nothing. This house was already here in 1895 and the old fairground was just up the street, but the land was sold after World War II and houses were built on it. Besides the county fair, traveling shows like circuses and carnivals set up on the fairground. It was actually pretty convenient for young Gadwell. When the circus came to what was then Thayerville, it was practically across the street from his own front door. All right, enough chit-chat. We'd better get a move on!"

"Just a moment," Mrs. Thayer said, coming into the dining room with a camera. "I want to get a picture first."

She had everyone pose for photos, both in a group shot that included everyone and a couple of variations. One had Grandpa, Mr. Thayer, Bill, Ryan, and Talitha representing four generations with five people (or maybe four, since one person was in it twice).

"We still have that pic!" Talitha exclaimed in astonishment when Mrs. Thayer showed it to her. "I never knew who everybody in it was until now!"

"*You're* in it," Ryan pointed out.

"I always thought that was Mom…"

Then there were admonitions to be careful and come back safely (to wherever each of them belonged) and farewell hugs. Mrs. Thayer hugged Bill especially warmly, to his obvious discomfort since he didn't even know the woman, and Ryan couldn't begin to sort out the mixed emotions going on there. He thought of those soldiers he had seen, but decided not to tell his mother that he didn't need to be reminded to be careful.

Not very silently fuming over what he saw as an unnecessary delay for trivial reasons, Grandpa finally hustled Ryan, Bill, and Talitha out the front door and into the cold night without even letting them put any coats on.

"We could do this in the house," he said to head off any objections, "but you'd have a heck of a lot of explaining to do to the relatives you scared the daylights out of when you popped up in their parlor."

He positioned the three in the snow of the front yard, facing each other at arm's reach as though at the points of an imaginary triangle.

"Stand back, everybody," he warned the others, who had followed them outside and were watching half curiously and half a little frightened. "I've never done this before and I don't quite know what might happen."

"That makes me feel a whole lot better," Ryan muttered as he shivered, holding his arms tightly against his chest. Talitha didn't seem to be bothered by the cold, but he wasn't wearing a self-heating jumpsuit like hers. "Couldn't I at least wear a coat?"

"You won't need a coat where you're going," Grandpa said.

"Funny," Ryan heard his father say to his mother. "That's what the minister told me at church last Sunday."

"Hey, good one!" Bill the Younger exclaimed. "I'll have to remember that!"

"This is no time for jokes!" Grandpa exclaimed to Mr. Thayer, then turned to the shivering threesome. "Now bump your rings together and shout 'Karlo!'"

They bumped fists and shouted "KARLO!" It sounded a little ragged, though, with Talitha's "Ow!" spoiling the effect somewhat. Nothing happened.

"Try it again," Grandpa said, "and this time say it together. One, two… three!"

They bumped fists once more. "KARLO!"

This time, it worked. It was as though they stayed in one place while

44

the world spun around them, as though they were in the center of a whirling circular ribbon of smeared color. Suddenly — it stopped.

Ryan looked around, blinking in the sudden bright sunlight. It was now a hot summer day with a clear blue sky overhead and no snow anywhere. The house at 128 was still there, looking much as it did before, though without any Christmas decorations. While there were now several empty chairs on the porch, seemingly made out of some kind of woven reed, no one was in sight, so their arrival had gone unnoticed. This far back, Ryan wasn't sure exactly what generation of relatives currently lived in the house. The trees in the front yard were in full leaf, including one that had long been cut down by Ryan's time. The other houses on either side weren't there yet and 128 stood by itself on a large expanse of grassy lawn. Behind it was a red barn and other outbuildings, an old-fashioned windmill, and open fields beyond. Some ways down the street, at the intersection with the highway, a large house with turrets stood on the corner. That was the MacEvoy house, gone in Ryan's time, still standing in Bill's time, and newly built here.

Out front, a horse and buggy went by in a cloud of dust. West Fairground Street wasn't even paved, just a dirt road cutting through the lush green cornfields that stretched seemingly uninterrupted to the hills in the distance, and the houses that would one day stand across the street were still long in the future. If he hadn't already known when he was supposed to end up, Ryan could have guessed the time of year to about the month from the height of the corn. "Knee-high by the Fourth of July" was the expression he'd heard, and it was even higher than that. And across the road and up a short distance was the fairground, where the huge tents of a circus had been set up.

"I think," Bill said in some awe, "we made it."

Chapter Seven

A huge banner at the entrance to the fairground announced

Colonel Waddell's Colossal Circus and Combined Traveling Show

in extravagant lettering with lots of serifs.

Circuses in the 1890s were low-tech entertainment, Ryan realized. Canvas tents were everywhere, and anything solid was made of wood and brightly painted. The Colonel included a "menagerie" among his attractions, which seemed to be a fancy word for a small zoo with exotic animals, and along with all the horses used for motive power, the odors on a hot day were amazingly rank. Talitha turned up her nose, making some muttered remark about the past being so dirty.

Other odors were more savory, and even though they had a job to do, they couldn't resist the small roasted peanut wagon and the bargain price of five cents per bag.

Only a few people were in sight, mostly circus workers like brawny roustabouts. Several male acrobats hurried past, wearing blue tights, red shorts, and blue shirts, and Ryan had to choke back a sudden urge to laugh out loud because they looked like Superman with a handlebar mustache. Judging by the sound of brassy music coming from the huge main tent, the afternoon show was in progress, which would explain where most of the paying customers were.

Suddenly somebody stood in front of Talitha, blocking her path. He was a tall, lean man of about forty with a waxed mustache and a pointed

COLONEL WADDELL

beard, wearing a Stetson hat and dressed like a cowboy, though with probably a lot more fancy fringe and spangles than working range-riders normally preferred.

He took a long, thin cigar out of his mouth and angrily drawled, "What're you doin' outside? You go on in ten minutes!"

Startled, Talitha almost dropped her bag of peanuts. "Go on what?"

The cowboy — who Ryan realized had to be none other than Colonel Waddell himself, since that was his face on all the posters and banners — looked at her more closely, then did a double take. What he made of her short hair was hard to tell, but she had enough of a figure showing through the jumpsuit to make it obvious she wasn't a boy.

"Beg your pardon, Miss," he mumbled, touching his leather-gloved fingers to the brim of his hat and lifting it slightly. "I thought you were one of the new bareback riders with that get-up! Sorry to've troubled you... enjoy the show!" He swaggered off, the spurs on his high-heeled boots jingling.

"Bareback riders...?" Talitha said puzzledly. "I don't get it."

"He means somebody who rides a horse without a saddle," Ryan replied. "Your clothes are from about 150 years from now, so he thought you were one of the performers in a costume."

Talitha glanced down at herself. "Costume? This is kinda normal for us. He was the one wearing the cowboy suit!"

Bill gave the main tent a longing gaze. "Wish we could stay and see the show."

Dad! "We're a little short on time you know." Looking around, Ryan saw the nearly deserted midway, a lane with facing rows of booths and small tents with games and sideshows. "Come on, I think it's over here."

The games of skill, like knocking down stacks of wooden milk bottles with a ball, were probably all crooked, and the freak show was doubtless tawdry and depressing. The Alligator Boy surely didn't look much like the painting on a banner that depicted some half-reptilian humanoid creature rising out of the swamp, more likely just an unfortunate kid with a rare skin condition that made him look like he was covered with scales.

What they were looking for, on the other hand, may have been the most authentic attraction of all, and they found it at the end of the row, a modest tent with a sign out front billing:

KARLO THE MAGNIFICENT! SEES ALL! KNOWS ALL!

The sign also featured a painting of a swarthy man with a black goatee and a fierce expression, wearing a turban and pointing his hands at a crystal ball while little thunderbolts came out of his eyes. A smaller sign by the entrance said **Admission 10¢,** but no one was around to collect the fee. The one person in sight, apparently a sideshow barker between shifts, was a couple of tents down, sitting on a wooden stool and reading a newspaper on a makeshift stage in front of a banner ballyhooing a sword swallower. His coat was off and he was in shirt and suspenders, but he still wore his derby.

He looked up. "Whadda you kids want?"

"We're looking for Karlo," Ryan said.

"His next show isn't till three," the barker answered curtly. "Come back then."

"We really need to talk to him," Ryan insisted. "Personally, I mean. He told us to come see him."

"Yeah?" The barker scratched his head. "I'll let him deal with you, then. You'll probably find him in his wagon back of the big top, but don't say I didn't warn you. He usually takes a nap about this time, and if you wake him up... well, you'd better be on the level, that's all I can tell you." He went back to his newspaper.

Behind the main tent and out of sight of the average ticket-buyer, they passed several rows of the horse-drawn wagons used in the circus parade, brightly painted with massive amounts of gold leaf and elaborate carvings. Although they were now deep in territory that should have been off-limits to outsiders and went by several circus workers busy with various jobs, no one tried to stop them. It occurred to Ryan that far from attracting unwanted attention, Talitha's red jumpsuit actually worked in their favor. Like Colonel Waddell himself, everyone who saw her would have assumed she and anyone with her must be part of the show.

Soon they found the 19th Century equivalent of a trailer park where all the drab wooden wagons in which the performers and crew lived had been lined up. Which one was Karlo's was impossible to tell at a glance, and they ended up asking an immensely obese woman just then rinsing out her dainties in a washtub outside her wagon (a sign on the side billed her as **"HALF-TON HARRIET, THE FATTEST FEMALE IN THE FORTY-FOUR STATES,"** not to mention the World's Weightiest Woman and the Peerless Pinnacle of Plump Pulchritude). She was friendly and cheerfully told them what they wanted to know, then she noticed

Talitha staring at her in undisguised horror.

"What is it, dearie?" she asked gently.

Talitha gulped. "Where I come from... we could cure you..."

Harriet smiled indulgently. "Maybe so, child, but then who would pay a dime to see me? This is how I make my living. And a good one, too. I travel, I meet people... I'm not complaining." She went back to her washing.

Talitha still stood there, still staring, and Ryan tugged at her arm to pull her away. "C'mon, we're on a mission, remember?"

On the way to Karlo's wagon and out of Harriet's hearing, Talitha suddenly burst out, "She was so... gaggly!"

"I think I almost understood that," Bill said. "You've never seen a fat lady before?"

"No!" Talitha blurted. "We don't *get* fat! It's in there with birth defects and disease and amputations, something horrible that people had to live with in the past but we don't because we can fix it!" She shuddered. "And people paid money to look at something like that...?"

"Squeamish." Bill shook his head. "And here I was all set to go take a look at the Alligator Boy..."

"Go right ahead, but I'm waiting outside!" Talitha exclaimed.

"People, we're in a hurry here..." Ryan reminded them.

By this time, they had made their way to a non-descript wagon somewhat to one side. The door was at the rear end, with a couple of wooden steps leading up to it.

Ryan mounted the steps and knocked, and after a moment they heard the sound of moving about within. Then the door opened a crack and a pair of burning eyes glowered at them from the dark interior.

"Who dares disturb the repose of Karlo the Magnificent?" intoned the attached sepulchral voice.

"Uh... we're from the future," Ryan said quickly, trying to get his explanation out before the magician closed the door on them, "and you sent for us..." He held up his hand to show him the ring.

Karlo raised one bushy eyebrow. "Oh, so it's you, is it? I knew you'd be coming sooner or later, but I certainly wasn't expecting children."

The door opened more widely, revealing the conjuror himself. He was a tall, thin, and swarthy man somewhere deep in middle age, wearing trousers with suspenders over a sleeveless undershirt, and worn slippers. He sported the black goatee shown in his poster, but without the turban he could be seen to be mostly bald on top.

He let them into his wagon. It was cramped and cluttered, with hardly enough room for one man, let alone four people, but they found seats on some dusty cushions on the floor. While Karlo may have been a powerful magician with genuine powers, he hadn't extended himself to tidying up his quarters. The wagon could have been the home of any older man living by himself, who saw no need to straighten up for company because he never had any and liked it that way. Besides some faded posters tacked to the walls that indicated he had once toured the Continent under the names "Karleau le Magnifique" and "Trollkarlo," the main hint that the wagon's occupant might be more than he seemed was a shelf over the rumpled cot-like bed. It was filled with old-looking books, large and thick with leather bindings, and Ryan wondered if they were spell books. "Grimoires" was the word he seemed to recall reading somewhere.

"You knew we were coming?" Bill asked.

"Yes, I sent a message to myself from the future to look for you," Karlo replied in a more matter-of-fact and not so theatrically affected tone. He still had a slight accent that suggested he hailed from foreign shores, but exactly where he was from Ryan couldn't tell. "You might call the process 'mental telegraphy,' and like telegrams, messages tend to be short and rather cryptic."

"Oh, it's like texting," Ryan said.

Bill looked blank. "Like what?"

"Oh, right, you used smoke signals way back when," Talitha said a little sniffily.

Karlo interrupted with a note of exasperation. "That being as it may, young people from afar... Please forgive me if I ask you to explain what this is all about and why you have made this remarkable journey across the abyss of time."

They introduced themselves and told their story, though Ryan wondered if Karlo was really able to follow it very well with all three trying to tell it at once or adding details and comments.

At one point, Karlo even interrupted Ryan with a rather testy-sounding, "Am I correct in assuming, my dear young fellow, that in your distant decadent age, the phrasing 'and he was like' is considered an indicator of direct discourse?" Seeing Ryan's baffled look, he added, "A signal that you are quoting someone's actual speech, analogous to 'he said'?"

Ryan could only nod. It hadn't been anything he had ever thought about, since that was how everyone he knew at school talked, and went on with his version of events. Meanwhile, Karlo sat cross-legged on his cushion in front of them and stared intently into a large crystal ball in his lap, now and then passing his hands over it. Although it glowed from within, what sense he could make of the swirling fog inside was hard to say. It just looked like a jumbo-sized snow globe to Ryan.

"I see..." Karlo said at the end of it, continuing to peer into the crystal ball. "The signs do indicate a massive disruption in the warp and woof of time and space stretching across three centuries. You did well to come to me, but then, I did send for you." He sighed and looked up. "As much as I dislike having to reveal secrets of the trade to non-initiates, I find I am compelled to admit that there is a darker sort of practitioner of the magical arts. I have had several unpleasant encounters with one in particular, known as Nechronus. Your description of events certainly corresponds with his manner of going about things. I am afraid your Uncle Gadwell did something extremely unwise by gathering children from different eras in a magical space outside of time, even though it was for something as innocuous as a Christmas party. By doing so, he inadvertently put you and the other children in a vulnerable position, and Nechronus took advantage of the opportunity to make an easy capture of everyone there in one fell swoop."

"He won't kill them, will he?" Ryan asked worriedly.

Karlo sat back and stared off into a distance only he could see through the wall of the wagon. "I very much doubt it. He would have other uses for them." After pondering a little more, he stood up. "There is no help for it, then. We shall have to journey to Nechronus's stronghold and rescue your compatriots."

"We?" Talitha exclaimed. "Can't you call the Magic Police or something?"

Karlo glowered at her as though thunderbolts were about to shoot out of his eyes like on his posters. "If there were such a thing, and there isn't, magicians like Nechronus would own it. Instead, there are guardians of order, of which I am one. When some catastrophe threatens to shatter the foundations of the natural world, it is my duty to act. Alone if I must, with deputized allies if I can obtain them. I may need assistance with locating and identifying the prisoners, and in the present circumstances, with so little time, you will just have to do. Besides, I was quite explicit in the message I sent myself. All three of you must accompany me in order to succeed in this endeavor. I wish I had thought to explain why, but I must assume I had good and sufficient reason."

"Why the hurry?" Ryan asked, thinking of some of the science fiction he had read, particularly the time-travel stories. "All this happened over a hundred years from now, right? You could take a year to round up some other magicians and still appear at the right moment to stop this Nechronus dude, couldn't you?"

"It is hardly that simple," Karlo said, his impatience obvious in his tone. "There is a master clock, you might say. If Nechronus abducted those children three hours ago, it is still three hours ago both for you and for him. Magic has its own rules, of which you are entirely unaware. On the other hand, Nechronus will not be expecting a response to his abduction so soon, and certainly not from such as yourselves."

"I certainly wouldn't," Talitha agreed.

"Speed is of the essence," Karlo then declared, "acting swiftly and resolutely before he has a chance to react. It is our only hope. Now out of the wagon with you. This will require a powerful spell and it would not be advisable to perform it in these confined quarters."

He urged them outside, then emerged from the wagon a couple of minutes later, having taken the time to dress. One simply did not confront wicked magicians in anything but formal attire, evidently. He had put on a shirt, a bow tie that he had actually tied instead of the clip-on sort that Ryan was familiar with, a vest, and a frock coat as well as his turban.

Karlo positioned them in something like a circle, with himself in the center, standing in the grass between wagons and blocked from view from anyone passing by along the main avenue.

"Now, if you are quite ready, we must be off." He raised a long black stick that looked like a magic wand and probably was one towards the sky and shouted some incomprehensible magic word.

The world began to spin around Ryan, even faster than it had during the first shift in time. *Here we go again*, he thought dismally.

"I think I'm gonna be sick—" Talitha started to squeal.

And then they were somewhere else.

Chapter Eight

They stood on a narrow, snow-covered path along a barren mountain-side. The wind was frigid and since Ryan didn't have a coat on, it seemed to cut straight through his body without stopping for anything on the way. Even with her heated suit, Talitha looked uncomfortable. Sheer rock faces were a nearly vertical wall towering over them on one side, a dizzying drop to unfathomable depths lost in the swirling mists below yawned on the other. In the distance, mountain peaks almost too jagged and pointed to be real were faintly visible in the hazy twilight. Above, the sky was a seething mass of gray clouds scudding along with the wind. What little sunlight penetrated them hardly made any difference in the gloom. Something flew overhead just then with a raucous squawk, too high and too obscured in the murk to make out very clearly, but it had bat-like wings and a pointed head with an overlong beak. More like a pterodactyl than a bird, Ryan thought.

About a mile or so ahead, at the end of the path winding in and out of view along the rock face, was a castle that rose from a mountain peak, all pointed towers and jagged battlements seemingly formed out of the glossy black rock itself rather than built on top. It looked more like a castle in a nightmare than an actual structure intended for real people to live in.

"Castle Nechronus," Karlo said in a near-whisper, as though he hated to say it out loud. "In all likelihood, the prisoners will be found somewhere within."

We're going up against the guy who built that? Ryan thought in dismay as he took in the castle, suddenly feeling colder than the wind alone could have made him.

"It does look... necrotic." Talitha hadn't actually gotten sick during the whirling transition, but her face was a little pale, as though it had been a near thing. "Where are we, anyway?" she added, glancing around at the surrounding mountains.

"In the world between the worlds," Karlo replied almost absently as he examined the rock wall along the path more closely, though Ryan still didn't feel as though the answer told him anything more than he knew before. "The Universe is far larger than you can envision, and here, in this desolate land outside of sidereal space and time, Nechronus has established his redoubt."

"So what do we do?" Bill asked. "Walk up to the front door and ring the bell?"

"Your humor is misplaced, young squire," Karlo said. "No, there are other ways, more direct ones, that will take us where we need to go."

He gestured with his wand. A pale blue light shone from the tip and played across the cliff face, and the rock wall next to them began to split apart. Massive columns of stone moved aside with a grating noise of rock grinding against rock, revealing the entrance to a tunnel leading into endless blackness.

"We could not materialize inside the citadel itself because it is too well-protected with magical defenses," Karlo explained, "but outside its confines, those of us keeping a watchful eye on Nechronus have located some clandestine entrances against the day we might need them. This is one such day. Now we must hasten inside before anyone notices us."

As soon as they were all in the tunnel, the entrance closed behind them. For a moment, the darkness around Ryan was absolute and he started to feel the beginnings of panic, then a light came on. Karlo was holding his wand up like a torch, its tip glowing a washed-out blue.

"I am loath to employ my wand in this manner," he said. "Although the magic I am using is slight, it can be perceived by entities sensitive to magical emanations. Our approach may be noticed by the wrong sort, but since we need the light, it is the lesser evil."

"Is that your problem?" Talitha asked. "Turn that thing off. We can use mine!" She snapped on the flashlight unit in her wristband.

As Karlo let the glow in his wand dim to nothing, it became clear that Talitha's light was brighter and more concentrated than his.

"These advances in the mechanical arts..." he muttered. "Soon no one will need magic at all. Very well, then. Lead the way, my dear."

With Talitha in front, they started into the darkness. The air in the tunnel was chilly and smelled stale, even musty, but at least inside the mountain they were out of the cold wind.

"If I didn't think this was all some kind of dream," Bill said as he walked along, "I'd be scared to death."

It did seem to Ryan that events had moved so fast that he had lost all touch with reality a while ago, and if he stopped to think about it, he would be a lot more scared than he actually was. Mostly he just felt numb, resignedly waiting to see what else would fall on him.

"Can we really just walk in here like this?" Talitha was asking Karlo. "If this Nehoozis is so powerful, won't he know we're here? You said he had magical defenses—"

"We are buried within so much solid rock that our presence cannot be detected if we refrain from using magic," Karlo assured her. "Unfortunately, Nechronus could still hear you were you close enough. The same applies to his guards, so it would be advisable to keep your voices down from this point on."

They walked for what seemed like miles through the tunnel, following Talitha's light ahead, with utter darkness all around and behind. The path was never straight for very long, always winding, twisting, and zig-zagging, and often the light was lost around the next bend. In places the roof was so low that they had to bend down. It was also narrow, with the cold, rough rock walls close on either side. Half-Ton Harriet never could have squeezed through, and at times Ryan felt as though he might have had some hard going himself if he weighed just a few pounds more. Other than for their footsteps on the rock floor, it was completely silent. As silent as a tomb, Ryan started to think, then decided he didn't like that comparison since his surroundings were too much like one in other ways. At a minimum, he was probably storing up material for a lifetime of nightmares.

It had been a very long day and he was starting to feel a little tired, but he kept going because he had to, and he tried not to think too much about what they might run into at the other end. He had to wonder, though. *Will we have to come back the same way?* More tired than he was now and herding freed prisoners with who knew what kind of pursuit at their heels?

Finally, they came to the end of the tunnel. In the light from Talitha's wristband, they saw a blank wall of rough stone blocks.

"Be ready," Karlo warned. "We are about to enter the lower levels of Castle Nechronus itself. There are doubtless seldom any guards this far down, but one never knows what might be lying in wait on the other side of a wall."

He pointed his wand at the stone blocks, murmuring a few words in some strange language. The tip of the wand glowed and the wall began to turn misty.

Be ready for what, Ryan had no idea. Nor did he have any clear notion of what he would do if, say, they broke into the kennel of a fire-breathing dragon the size of a Mack truck.

As he watched, an opening several feet wide and just tall enough to pass through opened up in the wall, leading to a wider passageway lined with smoothed stone and dimly lit by very occasional bluishly glowing globes mounted on the walls. After Talitha turned off her wristband, there was just barely enough light to see by. Karlo looked around warily as they came out of the tunnel but the corridor appeared to be deserted.

They stood there for a moment while Karlo got his magical bearings, and Ryan noticed that both his and Bill's clothes were fairly dirty from the long walk through the tunnel. Talitha's red jumpsuit was spotless, however, and even her boots and belt were still pure white. Something in the fabric that repelled dirt? It didn't extend to her skin, apparently, since one of her cheeks was smudged.

Karlo seemed satisfied after checking things out but still thought it necessary to remind them, "We might conceivably encounter a guard by sheer bad luck on our way, so stay alert!"

They followed him through a seemingly endless warren of corridors, up stone stairways, and through vast rooms. How Karlo knew where he was going was a mystery, but he led them onwards with every appearance of confidence.

Many rooms were luxuriously furnished but showed no signs that they had been used in a long time. The plumbing still worked, however, and when they paused for a long overdue break as well as to clean up a little, Karlo pronounced the clear, cold water that came from the bathroom faucets fit for human consumption.

At length they reached an intersection with another corridor. Motioning for the others to stand behind him a few paces, Karlo looked around the corner with all due caution.

"Aha!" he murmured and raised his wand.

An electric flash shot out with a loud crack, aimed at something in the intersecting corridor, then Karlo stepped past the corner and the others followed.

A little further along, in front of a massive-looking door, two stunned guards in black vinyl-like uniforms lay sprawled on the stone flooring, unconscious. The chrome helmet of one had fallen away and Ryan saw that the head underneath was far from anything human. His thought that he had seen a pig snout on the soldier in the party room earlier was at best only a rough approximation of the true horror. What he had taken for a snout was more like vastly enlarged insect mouth parts, and its huge, shiny black eyes were faceted, like a monstrous bug's. The rest of the body was more or less human in proportion and number of limbs, but that head... And since those enormous eyes didn't have lids, Ryan wondered how you could even be sure the guard really was unconscious.

Karlo stopped in front of the door. "I believe we have arrived at our destination. This would appear to be the place we seek." He probed the edges of the door with the tip of his wand. "Just as I thought. The defenses are light, more to keep the prisoners within than to withstand an assault from without. That is a good sign, as it means they are not expecting us."

He stood back, aimed his wand at the door, and shot a blue ray at the lock. It clicked and the door swung open. Karlo stepped inside and looked around, then motioned for the others to come on in after him.

Ryan had expected a castle dungeon that looked like a castle dungeon, with bare stone walls and rats running around, but this wasn't like that at all.

It looked more like a playroom for immensely rich and immensely spoiled children from around the year 1910. Besides being brightly lit, it was plushly carpeted and furnished with comfortable chairs and couches. Toys were everywhere. There were tables crowded with extravagant mechanical toys like merry-go-rounds and roller coasters, doll houses the size of cabinets, wall shelves full of board games, and stuffed animals and elaborately dressed dolls wherever they could find a space. The room was also decorated for Christmas with wreaths, garlands, and even several tinsel and ornament-bedecked trees, while a banner hung on the wall declared in large letters: "**WELCOME NEW FRIENDS!**" Somehow the festive holiday spirit fell a little flat in the circumstances.

Ryan didn't remember everybody from the Christmas party other than for a few standouts like Connor Walton, the '30s tough kid, and the pioneer girl in gingham, so it was hard to tell if anyone was missing, but just from the number of them all the kids seemed to be here. Instead of playing with the toys, they sat listlessly in the chairs or on the floor, staring into space or with their heads down. They looked up without much interest as Karlo and the others came into the room, probably not realizing this was a rescue party. If they had already met Nechronus, Karlo would have looked like just one more magician to them, and a rather sinister one at that.

"Did Nechronus do something to them already?" Ryan asked.

Karlo shook his head. "I think it more likely that they are merely depressed by their incarcerated situation. A prison furnished with toys is still a prison."

"Look, there's Mrs. G." Talitha pointed to a couch where Uncle Gadwell's wife sat with a bleak expression. "But I don't see *him* anywhere."

With Ryan and Talitha following, Karlo went over to her. Bill hung back, fascinated by some baseball equipment lying on a table, like a bat, ball, and glove, though whether there was a place to actually play within Castle Nechronus was a good question.

Ryan saw Bill pick up the bat in a two-handed grip, eye it critically, and give it a practice swing. *Dad, we're on a mission here...!* With a sigh,

Ryan turned back to Karlo and Mrs. Gadwell.

"Where is Gadwell Thayer?" Karlo was asking her.

"They took him..." Mrs. Gadwell said lowly. "The guards took him away." She shuddered at the thought, then added, "We were put here and told to wait until Nechronus himself has time to deal with us, as he is occupied at the moment."

"Ah, luck is in our favor, then," Karlo said, a little too optimistically in Ryan's opinion. "That will gain us the time we require to—"

"PUT HANDS UP!"

Ryan, Talitha, and Karlo whirled. Behind them, a guard in a chrome helmet had appeared seemingly out of nowhere. He held up a truncheon, something like a nightstick two feet long with a grip on one end and on the other a pair of electrodes that crackled with blue electric sparks, and pointed it at them.

Karlo reacted instantly, firing a bolt of lightning from his wand at the guard. Not that it did any good. The guard was protected by an invisible shield. A shimmering, semi-transparent bluish hemisphere several feet in diameter and centered on the truncheon's electrodes lit up when the magical bolt hit it, as though absorbing the energy and deflecting it harmlessly. Whatever else the truncheon did, it kept even a magician armed with a magic wand at bay. Perhaps that was what it had been designed for, to put non-magical guards on something like an equal footing with enemy magicians with wands.

"Drop wand, too!" the guard added to Karlo for good measure, in a guttural, rasping voice.

Karlo hesitated but looked stymied, as though he realized he had no choice.

Too intent on glaring at them with his huge, bulging, unblinking faceted eyes, the guard didn't realize that Bill was a little in back of him and holding a baseball bat. Bill gave the bat another practice swing, then stepped up to an imaginary plate behind the guard, took a deep breath, and swung the bat as hard as he could against the back of the guard's head. The protective field didn't extend to the rear, and the bat slammed into the helmet with a loud clang. Bill staggered back a step, looking as though the impact had recoiled painfully into his hands.

His brain protected by the helmet and a hard-shelled head, the guard was barely even stunned, but it did get his attention. He started to turn to deal with this new annoyance, making the mistake of pointing his truncheon away from Karlo.

With a loud crack, lightning shot across the room from Karlo's wand and briefly engulfed the guard's body in a blue electric storm. The guard stiffened, then fell over forwards and lay there on the floor, arms and legs twitching feebly while the truncheon he had carried rolled away from his limp fingers. Ryan bent down and picked it up, careful not to touch the electrodes still crackling with sparks. He didn't know exactly how the truncheon worked, but just having it made him feel a little better, just as Bill obviously felt more confident hefting the baseball bat.

"That should hold him a little longer." Karlo allowed Bill one of his rare smiles. "Well done, young squire."

"That was awesome, Da— Bill!" Ryan added. "You rock!"

Bill beamed. He may not have understood exactly what Ryan had said, but he took it as a compliment.

"But where did that bug-guy come from?" Talitha wondered. "He kinda popped up out of nowhere."

"I would tend to think he was one of the pair that were posted outside the door," Karlo said. "I must not have hit him with a strong enough charge the first time."

"Then where's the other one?" Ryan went across the room to the door and looked out. The corridor was deserted in both directions. "He's gone!"

"He must have run off to sound the alarm." For the first time, Karlo sounded a little worried. "That means we haven't much time after all. Ryan, watch out the doorway for any signs of oncoming foes."

"You here to get us out?" one of the kids asked.

"Indeed we are!" Karlo exclaimed. "Everybody," he announced to the room as a whole, "gather 'round!"

After watching what had just happened in complete bafflement, the kids in the room now realized that they were being rescued, and they lost all their indifference. There was an excited buzz and chatter and some questions as they stood up, but Karlo urged them to silence.

"We aren't going back through the tunnel, are we?" Talitha asked anyway.

"It would take too long," Karlo said, "and Nechronus could overtake us before we could reach the end. Fortunately, being inside his wall of magical defenses, we are not limited to physical means of egress. Stand back, everyone."

He pointed his wand at the wall. A blue radiance spread across the paneling, dissolving it, and an archway about eight feet wide took shape, opening onto the endlessly long, door-lined hallway outside the party room that Ryan remembered from before.

"Now then, through here," Karlo instructed the kids. "Remain there until someone comes for you."

With some murmuring but mostly just a lot of relief, the kids shuffled through the archway and into the corridor.

Karlo nodded to Mrs. Gadwell, who was standing by as the last of the kids slipped through past her. "You too, Madame."

"But my husband—" she said anxiously.

"We'll see to him," Karlo promised, and she reluctantly followed the kids into the hallway. "Don't let them open any doors," he called after her. "There is no telling where they might end up, and the odds are that none will be the right ones anyway."

"I understand," Mrs. Gadwell replied. "Please find my husband!"

"Have no fear of that," Karlo assured her, and turned to Bill and Talitha. "Now you as well."

Bill looked at Talitha and she nodded. "Can't we stay and help you?" Bill then asked.

Standing in the doorway, Ryan could only admire his father-to-be's courage, if not his common sense, when he had a chance to get away while the getting would never be any better.

"I haven't the time to argue," Karlo said sternly. The archway was already starting to close from each end, with wall gradually appearing in place of open space. "From this point on, however, the danger will be immense. Only a powerful and experienced magician can stand up to Nechronus and rescue Gadwell, and so I must go alone. You would only be a hindrance for me after this. This matter is not subject to disputation. Now get in there, all of you, before the portal closes—"

A blinding burst of blue flame exploded in the center of the room. Ryan was all but thrown out into the corridor by the blast of displaced hot air. Coming to a staggering stop in the doorway, he looked back to see what had happened.

Grim and terrifying, a human figure took shape in the eruption of blue fire and inky black smoke. It could only be Nechronus himself, tall and wearing a silken black robe embroidered with moving silver threads that formed ever-shifting occult patterns. His face was mostly hidden by a large shaggy ruff at his neck and a smooth, featureless, chrome-gleaming mask, but his blazingly intense eyes could be seen through a pair of narrow slits.

"You dare enter my own sanctum and interfere with my private matters?" Nechronus demanded in a rumbling voice that shook the walls, not from loudness but from some undertone of sheer sonic force.

"Abduction of innocent children is not a private matter," Karlo replied coolly, "and your imprisonment of a fellow magician cannot be tolerated."

"He was a fool engaged in an activity no less unsanctioned," Nechronus retorted, "and you were a fool as well to come here. Now pay the price!"

The room was suddenly filled with deafeningly roaring bolts of lightning as Nechronus attacked. Karlo had sensed it coming and responded almost instantly. They were immediately hidden by vast billowing clouds of blue and black smoke shot through with a barrage of electric discharges.

Gasping and choking on the smoke filling the room, Ryan stumbled out into the corridor to get away from the firestorm. Through a thin spot in the smoke, he could see a squad of guards approaching from down the corridor. He still held the truncheon he'd taken off the guard, but he certainly couldn't fight a mob of bug-men by himself. He couldn't go back into the playroom, either, at least not without being incinerated by a stray bolt of lightning.

With no other choices and a feeling of panic settling in, he turned and ran in the opposite direction, retracing the route Karlo had followed to reach the playroom. The intersection with the other corridor was only a short distance away and once he was around the corner, he was out of the oncoming guards' sight. He just hoped they hadn't seen him through the smoke.

Chapter Nine

Some time later, Ryan was too exhausted to go any further. He stopped to catch his breath, sinking to the floor with his back against the wall in a particularly dark pool of shadow. After running down so many dimly lit corridors, turning so many corners, cutting through so many dark rooms, going up and down so many different stairways, he had no idea where he was in relation to the playroom, or even whether he was on the same level with it. All he knew for certain was that he was now completely lost.

On the other hand, he was still free and he was armed, for all the good a weapon he didn't know to use might do him. He did find the switch on the handle that turned it off so he wouldn't accidentally burn himself, but that was about the only progress in anything that he had made so far.

Ryan doubted if Nechronus had lost the fight. If Karlo had won, he would have immediately started looking for him so they could all go home and would have found him by now. Instead, Ryan was alone in the dark, silent corridors, and time was continuing to tick away without any hint of help arriving very soon.

Besides, Karlo had gone head to head with a magician whose powers were at least on a par with his own, and on that magician's home turf. The odds wouldn't have been good in any event. Most likely, assuming he had lived through the battle, Karlo was now a prisoner somewhere, along with Bill and Talitha. Ryan didn't want to even think about the alternative possibilities, like what he would do if Karlo had been killed. Bad as that prospect was, since only Karlo could get him home, something happening to Bill would be far worse, since that would mean he would never be born — never would have been born — or whatever the darned verb tense was.

Ryan looked down at his hands. They were still there, as solid as ever. At least he wasn't fading out of existence, which was a good sign.

This just wasn't supposed to happen. The rescue mission had turned into a disaster. Even though they had gotten the rest of the kids out of the castle, now the rescue party itself was stuck here. Not only that, the rescued kids still weren't home yet, and were waiting in that corridor with all the doors for somebody to come get them. Only Karlo even knew where they were.

With a sick feeling of complete helplessness, Ryan realized it had all come down to him. And he had no idea what to do next.

He tried to think it through. *If I got out of this, I'd remember how helpless I felt, and I'd come back as a grown-up and get me out of it.*

He peered hopefully into the darkness along the empty corridor.

No one appeared out of nowhere in the gloom.

Maybe I didn't get out of it...? But if I didn't, where did Talitha come from? Or is she about to fade away like she never happened?

As he sat there and wrestled with the problem, it began to dawn on him that the situation wasn't entirely hopeless.

The bug-men didn't seem to have noticed his escape in the smoke, so as far as he could tell, nobody was after him. For that matter, Nechronus probably didn't even know he existed, and wouldn't be ordering his minions to search for him. That meant Ryan was not only still free but free to move around.

The castle was huge but not infinite. Bill, Talitha, and Karlo all had to be somewhere. Finding them seemed like the logical first step. It was the only thing he could do, actually. He certainly wasn't going home on his own without Karlo.

Thinking about it, he reasoned that they probably would have been locked up while Nechronus decided what to do with them. He doubted if they would be kept anywhere as nice as that playroom after what had happened, and if this was like any castle Ryan had ever read about, there had to be a dungeon somewhere. All he had to do was find it. How he would get them out was a problem he would worry about once he saw how the land lay.

Ryan got back to his feet and started off again. Having something definite to do already made him feel better. He even seemed to be getting something like a second wind, and no longer felt tired.

He followed the corridors and went up several flights of stone stairs. Along the way, he kept an eye out for anything that looked like it might be a dungeon, but nothing obvious turned up.

When he reached the ground-floor level and approached an intersection with another corridor, a girl crossed the open space in front of him. She was about Ryan's age and wearing a black maid's costume with a frilly white apron and white cap. Ryan froze for a second, wondering if she would sound the alarm when she saw him. But the girl just walked past, apparently too occupied with thinking about whatever her errand was to even glance at him.

Maybe he was less conspicuous than he thought. He held the truncheon out of sight against his side and under his arm, and went around the corner.

This hallway was wider and better lit than the others had been, though the natural light coming through the high arched windows was still fairly dim due to the cloudy skies outside. Unlike the playroom, no effort to deck the halls for Christmas had been made. The only attempt at decoration was the boldly emblazoned letter **N** carved in the stonework at frequent intervals. Somebody had gone to some effort to make sure no one forgot who was in charge here.

Ryan soon passed other people, but not many. Even in its more populated districts, the castle seemed so overwhelmingly vast compared to the relatively few inhabitants that he wondered if Nechronus had taken it over by no doubt foul means from much more numerous previous occupants. More striking was the fact that everyone he saw was about the same age, fourteen or fifteen, maybe sixteen at the outside. Most were outfitted in uniforms, such as girls in maids' costumes and boys in servants' livery, but a few were casually dressed in the clothing of a variety of different eras. Overall, it looked like a low-rent school play with kids not very convincingly stuck in adult roles. None paid any attention to Ryan as they went by.

Then a squad of half a dozen bug-men guards appeared ahead, led by a human officer in a bright red jacket with golden epaulets and a lot of braid. If he'd been more inclined to see the humor in the situation, Ryan would have thought the officer looked amazingly like the drum major leading the Centerpoint High School marching band in the parade he had seen in what now seemed like a very distant world an awfully long time ago. As they approached, Ryan felt as though he was sweating ice cubes, but tried to look as though he was on his way somewhere with some purpose in mind. He shuffled along with lowered eyes, not even looking at the guards as they went by. The guards in turn ignored him and continued on their way.

Ryan started to feel a little relieved. *Of course! If you're the right age, they just assume you belong here.* It was like his old school. He had known most of the kids at least on sight, but there were so many that he wouldn't have noticed a new face in the halls right off.

The next few windows he passed looked out on a snow-covered interior courtyard surrounded by the castle's high black walls and soaring towers. It was a cemetery with rows of plain gravestones under the gray sky, and near the windows where the snow had been cleared were some graves that looked freshly dug.

Wait a second! Ryan told himself after the first shock passed. If Nechronus was killing people left and right for the fun of it, he'd get rid of the bodies so no one would ever find them. This was too much out in the open. It must have meant that the castle had been here for a long time and the people who lived in it didn't live forever any more than other people did. But if people were dying naturally of old age, where were the old people? There didn't seem to be an obvious answer, or at least he couldn't think of one.

He came to a stairway leading downwards, and the lower level seemed as good a place as any to look for the dungeon. He passed several people but no one thought to stop him as he went down the stone steps.

Below, the stairway ended on a corridor dimly lit by blue globes at long intervals, and after a few minutes of exploring he found the dungeon down a narrow side corridor. A lone bug guard armed with the usual truncheon stood outside a heavy door in a pool of pale bluish light shed by one globe on the ceiling. As with the playroom, the guard was probably just there to keep the prisoners in. No one would have expected an enemy to penetrate so deeply within the castle. That was how Ryan hoped the reasoning went, anyway.

Unfortunately, the corridor came to a dead end just past the dungeon. There was no way to pretend he just happened to be walking past on some legitimate errand. The dungeon was a place people went to on purpose or they wouldn't be going down that corridor at all.

Guess I'll just have to bull my way through...

He walked towards the dungeon door, pretending to have every good reason for being there. His confidence that the ploy would work wasn't very high, but he tried not to let it show and held the truncheon just behind his back.

"What you want?" the guard rasped as Ryan came up to him.

"I'm supposed to make sure the prisoners are secure," Ryan replied, repeating something he'd heard in a movie and hoping it sounded suitably official and that his voice didn't crack from sheer nervousness, as well as trying to get over his sheer amazement that something like this bug-thing actually talked and that he could talk to it.

The guard clicked his mandibles, seemingly a little at a loss. "Never problem before." He tapped a ring of large metal keys hanging from his belt. "Me keymaster. Nobody get out unless I unlock door."

Good to know, Ryan thought and whipped out the truncheon. He snapped it on, the electrodes at the end lit up with crackling sparks, and he pressed the trigger. A bolt of lightning shot out with an electric crack and engulfed the guard.

Not anticipating any treachery since every kid in the place would have been assumed to be on the Nechronus team, the guard was too slow to react and went down in a flurry of waving arms and legs, and lay twitching on the stone floor. Relieved that he hadn't fumbled with the truncheon or dropped it outright at the critical moment, Ryan switched it off. He was also relieved that he hadn't killed the guard, but the discharge had probably played havoc with his nervous system, or whatever man-sized bugs had, and hopefully would keep him out of action for a good while.

Ryan removed the key ring from the guard's belt, and started trying out the various keys on the door lock. After two or three failed attempts, one finally worked and the door came open with a rusty creak as he pulled on the handle.

He stepped through the doorway. Inside, the dungeon was more like what he would have expected of a detention center in a creepy old castle, as opposed to the playroom elsewhere, with bare stone walls and floor, and some rude cots, lit by a single faint blue globe in the ceiling. The room was large enough to hold several people, and though Karlo wasn't there, Ryan saw Bill and Talitha sitting on their cots. They had looked up worriedly as the door opened, then their faces brightened when they saw who was coming in.

Bill leaped up and clapped Ryan on the back. "Boy, am I glad to see you!"

"Not half as glad as I am to see you," Ryan was quick to point out.

"And I'm glad to see both of you," Talitha added.

"You missed all the fun," Bill told him. "Karlo and Nechronus started throwing lightning bolts at each other. Really tore the room apart. I think Nechronus was extra p.o.'ed because all the toys got blown up."

"I'm surprised *you* weren't blown up," Ryan said. "It looked like a real firestorm in there."

Talitha nodded. "It was. We dove for cover real quick. Got a little singed, though…" she added, glancing at a mild burn on the back of her hand.

"Anyway," Bill went on, "Nechronus won in the end. I guess he was just a more powerful magician. I don't think Karlo got killed, but the last we saw of him, he looked like he was in pretty bad shape and a couple of the bug-boys were carrying him off somewhere. Then Nechronus found us and said that with all the rest of his prisoners gone we'd just have to do instead. So we've been cooling our heels in here ever since, I guess waiting for somebody to get around to us."

"Spare some of your self-pity for me," spoke up another voice, from a cot further back in the shadows. "I've been here three full days, not merely an hour."

It wasn't just Bill and Talitha in the dungeon. There was also a boy, slender and blond, wearing a coarse shirt, rather baggy pants, and worn buckled shoes that hadn't been polished for a very long time.

"This is Thomas, the stable master around here," Talitha said, and Ryan did notice a horsey whiff coming from the boy's direction. "He's from about 1790 and Nechronus stuck him in here to punish him for something megaloco like being too slow to follow an order or not smiling like he meant it while he did it. Anyway, Thomas told us some interesting things. How old do you think he is?"

It seemed like an abrupt change of subject, but Ryan answered. "Sixteen, maybe?"

Thomas smiled sadly. "Thirty-two, last birthday."

Ryan did a double take. "What?"

Thomas nodded. "Aye, 'tis the truth, and I'll swear to it on a stack of Bibles. Great Master Nechronus lures folk into his service by dangling the bait of eternal youth. Indeed, we never age whilst we are here... outwardly. Within our bodies, however, the clock continues to tick, and eventually we die of old age even with the appearance of youth. It is further whispered that our lives are shortened thereby, that forestalling the ravages of age consumes us more quickly than otherwise. The Master, of course, told us none of this when he engaged us, and once we are here, none may change his mind or protest too loudly. There has been occasional rebellion nonetheless, but the guards quickly put down any unrest."

"We think that's what this is all about," Talitha added. "A lot of people have died lately and Nechronus is getting a little short-handed." (*Those new graves!* Ryan thought.) "He can't just kidnap kids from Earth against their will, or he'd have problems with other magicians. So he usually has to lure kids here with false promises and make it all seem sort of voluntary. That playroom with all the toys was part of it, at least as bait for younger kids. 'Join me and you can play with all these spiffin' toys whenever you want!' Once you sign up, though, it's a different story. 'Here's a bucket and a mop! Get to work!' Those toys didn't look like they'd ever been played with."

"That guard I beaned walked right by me while I was holding a baseball bat," Bill put in. "I don't think he had a clue what it could be used for."

"But it's a lot of work conning kids into signing up of their own free will," Talitha continued. "When Uncle Gadwell threw his little party in a place that wasn't exactly on Earth, the kids weren't protected any more, and Nechronus could grab a whole bunch of new slaves at one time without having to go to the trouble of recruiting volunteers."

Things were falling into place, but an obvious question occurred to Ryan. "What about the big guy himself? Shouldn't he be hundreds of years old? What keeps him going while everybody else dies of old age?"

Thomas shrugged. "Many of us have wondered that very thing. We suppose that the Master uses some manner of magic on himself that is denied his followers, but no one knows for certain. He does have some few favorites, bootlicking lackeys, and they may be preserved as well, but such is not for the common sort."

"But what's the whole point of this place?" Ryan asked. Maybe they were wasting valuable time talking like this, but he had to find out what was going on in order to figure out what to do next. "Why does he keep everybody young like that?"

"Very little is known for certain," Thomas admitted, "but when we are out of earshot of the guards and the lackeys, we do talk amongst ourselves and exchange such scraps of information as we have overheard. Perhaps what I tell you now is merely rumor, but..."

Put in some kind of logical order, the fragments of gossip suggested that as a young boy on the mundane plane a long time ago, Nechronus had been mocked by the other children for being a bookish grind. The mockers had no idea that the books the fat and solitary boy studied so intently were really books of magic that soon gave him a terrible power, which he immediately used to get his revenge on his tormenters. Eliminating the original mockers was not enough, however, and he *kept on* getting his revenge as the years rolled into decades and then centuries, with new generations of young people he just *knew* would have mocked him if they had been given the chance. Castle Nechronus, where he ruled supreme over trembling and fearful slaves the same apparent age of those who had once ridiculed him, was the result. Some part of Nechronus's mind had apparently been frozen in time at the moment of his humiliation, and he could never get past it.

"This guy's got some serious issues," Ryan concluded at the end of it, then realized how much time had been passing while they talked. "But that's his problem. Ours is getting Karlo and Gadwell out of this so they can send us home."

Thomas looked at him with sudden hope shining in his eyes. "Then you are here to rescue all of us who are held in captivity? It's what we've dreamed of for so many years, but we never knew how it could be done!"

Rescue? Everyone in the castle? Ryan had a feeling that things were spinning rapidly out of control. As far as he knew, Karlo had never intended more than extracting the dozen-plus kids who had been at the party, but now a whole mob?

Not wanting to promise a lot more than he could deliver, Ryan just went with the flow and said, "Well, that's up to our friend Karlo, but I don't see why not... We have to find Karlo first, though."

"I think I know where your friend must be," Thomas said, "for it is where the Master performs his most evil deeds. It is an unholy place but I can lead you there if you wish."

Ryan didn't care for the "evil" or the "unholy" parts, but it wasn't as though he had a choice after coming this far.

On the way out, Bill scooped up the unconscious guard's truncheon, then they dragged the bug-man inside the cell and locked the door on him. With any luck, it would all be over by the time he came to, but if he did revive a little prematurely, he wouldn't be able to sound the alarm. Not taking care of that little detail had been their mistake back at the playroom and led to their present predicament, and it seemed like a good idea not to repeat it.

With Thomas leading the way, they went along more corridors and up and down more staircases. After perhaps ten minutes, Thomas stopped in front of a large set of closed wooden double doors.

"In here," he said, then announced, "As for me, I shall go seek others who oppose Great Master Nechronus and bring them to your aid. The time has come to overthrow this tyranny once and for all!" He turned and trotted down the corridor.

"Can't say as I blame him," Bill said, watching Thomas disappear around a corner, "but I just want to go home."

Ryan opened one of the doors carefully, trying to be as quiet as possible, and looked inside. On the other side of the doorway was a balcony overlooking a vast semicircular amphitheater below, unlit except for a stage at the far end. The ceiling arched high overhead, lost somewhere in the gloom. It reminded him of his school auditorium, only much larger and much darker. It was definitely a place he would have preferred to be coming out of rather than going into, but he went on inside anyway and the others followed.

On the brightly spotlit stage and surrounded by darkness stood gigantic masses of machinery like transformers, generating huge crackling arcs of blinding bluish-white electricity. Off to one side and dwarfed by the rumbling colossuses towering over them, a couple of technicians in white lab coats worked at a desk-sized instrument panel straight out of a NASA control room, filled with illuminated dials, knobs and switches, video screens, and lights blinking in blue, red, and green. If sufficiently advanced science looked like magic, this was advanced magic that looked like science.

In the center of the lighted area were two tables that resembled hospital operating tables — or maybe dissecting tables was a better comparison — connected to each other and the enormous banks of machinery behind them by tangled masses of thick cables.

"He's got Karlo and Uncle Gadwell strapped to those tables," Talitha whispered.

How can she see anything from this far away? Ryan thought, then saw that she was holding her hand up and looking at a little square lighted video image on her wristband. *No wonder she thought a phone with a camera was "old stuff!"*

Looking more closely at the image, Ryan saw that the shackles holding the magicians' wrists glowed a pale green, suggesting something magical about them, perhaps inhibiting the use of their power. Gadwell was struggling weakly against the straps, while on the table next to him, Karlo lay still, apparently unconscious. Nechronus himself paced between the tables, his robe rippling and flowing with each sweeping motion. Ryan noticed that Nechronus strode a little stiffly, as though his knees weren't working right.

They could hear Nechronus taunting Gadwell in a booming voice that filled the vast room and echoed from the walls and ceiling even though it was muffled by the mask he wore.

"You had the temerity to defy me in the Council, Gadwell. I cannot let that go unanswered. By the time of the next Council, your voice will not be heard to oppose my will. Indeed, your minuscule amount of power shall have been added to mine, and what became of the dried-up husk that once housed your feeble wits will be a mystery that no one will ever solve!"

"You won't get away with this, Nechronus!" Gadwell tried to exclaim, though he was so weak that it came out as a faint wheeze from a speaker on the wristband.

"No? There is no one to rescue you now that Karlo is my prisoner as well, and what an unexpected prize he was! Now I have two magicians whose power I can absorb. With so much power, I shall be the mightiest of all and no one on the Council will ever dare to challenge me again." Nechronus laughed nastily. "Reflect on that in these last few minutes that remain to you!"

"But don't you realize your scheme can't possibly work?" Gadwell protested feebly. "The Karlo you have is from before I became his apprentice! If you destroy him now, I could not be here!"

"Merely a minor eddy in the river of Time," Nechronus said with oozing contempt, "and simple enough to allow for with but a slight correction or two. But I thank you for bringing it to my attention!" He whirled in a flurry of his rustling cape and stalked out of the pool of light in the center of the room, moving something like an arthritic stork.

There was no time to wait for help from Thomas. Nechronus was about to do something terrible to both Karlo and Gadwell, and Ryan couldn't let it happen if he wanted to go home. "We've got to get down there."

"Right behind you," Bill said, trying to sound more cheerful than he probably felt. Talitha just looked resigned to things getting worse than they already were.

They went back out into the corridor and a little further along came to a stairway that led downwards. On the next level, they found a curving corridor that ran along the outer wall of the amphitheater. The wall was blank and featureless most of the way, but finally they came to another set of massive doors.

The doors upstairs that led to the balcony had not been guarded, but here a single bug sentry had been posted. He saw them coming but didn't react at first, as usual most likely assuming that they were just more slaves with a reason for being there and that they would walk on by. His job was probably merely to make sure that whatever was going on inside wasn't accidentally interrupted by a cleaning crew or anyone else with a perfectly innocent reason to go in.

They had intended to spring their truncheons on him before he realized anything was wrong, but perhaps they approached him too closely, rousing his suspicions.

He already had his truncheon out as they came up, rasping, "Who you? What you do here?" Sparks crackled from the electrodes at the tip, and he pointed it threateningly at them. "Nobody allowed here when Master renew himself!"

Ryan and Bill looked at each other. Now what? The guard knew how to use his truncheon and they barely knew how to turn theirs on. Even at best, the protective energy shield projected by the truncheons probably made it difficult for opponents both armed with them to gain a clear advantage. It was a standoff, and all the bug had to do was call for help—

"Hey, Bugface!" Talitha suddenly yelled. Startled, the guard glanced at her, and she shone the pencil-thin, concentrated light beam from her wristband straight into his compound eyes. He screeched like metal being ripped apart and fell back, dropping his truncheon and clutching at his eyes. Ryan leaped forward and knocked the guard out with a bolt from his own truncheon.

"Good job, kid," Bill told Talitha. "What made you think that would work, though?"

Talitha shrugged. "I just figured that with those big eyes, they've got to be pretty sensitive to light, and that might be why the lighting in the corridors is kept so dim. So a bright light would probably be like a laser beam hitting him."

Ryan stared at her in amazement. *I never would have thought of that. How did she get all the family brains?* Maybe Kelsey had contributed more to the mix than he would have thought. She did get better grades than he did...

They opened the doors just enough to slip through inside the vast, dark amphitheater, hoping no one down in the center would notice the slight crack of light, and dragging the unconscious bug-man inside with them so no one chancing by in the corridor would find his prone body and call for backup.

Keeping low in the darkness, they slipped down the sloping aisle between concentric rings of seats. Perhaps the previous owners of the castle had used this room for concerts or plays, but Ryan doubted if Nechronus cared to provide entertainment for his subjects. His slaves served him, not vice versa. Now the amphitheater was used for other purposes, with the center filled with all that strange machinery.

Trying to stay hidden in the shadows, they crept closer to the stage, and paused at the edge. Before them was the same scene they had viewed from the balcony above, but now on the same level they were. The lab-coated technicians working at the control panel were just a few yards away, unaware they were being watched.

Bathed in a fountain of shimmering rainbow-colored light, Nechronus himself sat motionless on an elevated throne that was connected by cables to the surrounding machinery and to the tables where Gadwell and Karlo were lying. Stretched out on a third table was a new addition, a grossly fat boy of about fourteen.

Ryan thought he could guess what was going on. Nechronus intended to drain Karlo and Gadwell of their magical power while the overly nourished boy would provide youth and vitality to keep the old magician going for a few more decades. Recalling Nechronus's threat about dried-up husks, Ryan doubted if there would be much left of the kid when this was done. *One more to rescue*, he thought tiredly.

From the way Nechronus's head lolled on his chest, Ryan suspected that he wasn't even conscious at the moment. That meant Nechronus was at his most vulnerable right now. They would never have another chance like this.

He motioned to Bill and Talitha. "I'll take care of the guys in lab coats. See if you can get Gadwell and Karlo loose."

With a dismal feeling that he was committing himself and there was no way they could turn back now, Ryan clambered onto the stage.

The technicians looked up as he approached. Like everyone else in the castle, they appeared young, no more than sixteen. Standing in their lab coats in front of the control board, they gave Ryan the impression of a science fair project gone very bad.

"What are you doing here?" one demanded in annoyance bordering on outrage. "You know no one is permitted inside the Grand Hall during the Master's treatment! Leave at once or I'll call the guards!"

There wasn't time to think of lame excuses to justify being there, and Ryan didn't bother, whipping out his truncheon and pulling the trigger.

Both technicians went down in a storm of blue lightning and sprawled on the floor. After a quick glance to reassure himself that he hadn't killed them, since human beings might be less tolerant to electrical firestorms than bugs, Ryan went to work on the control panel, smashing dials with his truncheon and pulling out wires, hoping that wrecking the controls would stop the energy absorption process and make rescuing the prisoners easier and safer. It was probably superficial vandalism at best, but it seemed to have some effect: control lamps blinked out, overhead lights flickered, the rumble of motors ground to a halt.

Out the corner of his eye, he could see Bill and Talitha busy freeing Gadwell and Karlo, but he mostly watched for any reaction from the unconscious form of Nechronus in the chair. Having an awakened and no doubt very angry evil magician on their necks before Karlo and Gadwell were back in shape would be disastrous, but there was still no sign of any stirring from the figure in the chair.

Once he had done about as much damage as he could, he ran to the table where the fat boy lay under a spray of colored light and yanked out the cables. The lights flashed, flickered, and died away. Unlike Karlo and Gadwell, the kid had not been strapped down and sprawled there nearly naked, wearing only something like dingy boxer shorts, unconscious but writhing as though in pain and moaning softly. He had a greasy mop of long black hair and pale white skin that hadn't seen sunlight for a long time. He apparently hadn't seen a bathtub for a while, either, but Ryan could hardly blame him for that. Nechronus probably wasn't one to waste little luxuries like hygiene or regular exercise on prisoners whose life energy he intended to absorb. The boy may have even been used before, as there were several patches and plug-ends embedded in his chest and neck that looked like connectors for tubes or wires.

Ryan tried to drag the kid off the table and get him on his feet. "C'mon!" he urged. "Wake up! You're free but we've get to get out of here!"

The kid started to show some signs of returning awareness, just enough to open his eyes and look around without much comprehension.

Bill and Talitha had pried Gadwell and Karlo loose from their res-pective tables in the meantime and were trying to move them in Ryan's direction, apparently assuming the fat kid's table must be the rallying point. Neither magician looked exactly well. Karlo was still unconscious and Bill had to hold him upright while trying to drag him over, while Gadwell was hardly in any better shape, leaning heavily on Talitha as though he was about to ooze to the floor at any moment. The energy-draining process had probably gone on just long enough to knock a lot out of him.

This isn't good, Ryan thought. His plan had required at least one fully functioning magician to teleport everybody out of the castle and out of Nechronus's reach, preferably to that hallway of time so all the other kids could be sent home as well. But neither of the only two available magicians looked as though he would be up to anything like that very soon. Hiding somewhere in the castle until Karlo or Gadwell came around enough to do some serious magic didn't look like a good option, either, at least not if they had to drag three barely conscious ex-prisoners through corridors where bug guards would be coming along at any moment.

Ryan glanced nervously at Nechronus on the throne. Still no reaction. The figure still sat there, still wrapped in the surrounding glow, still apparently unconscious. That was fine for the moment, but who knew how long that happy state of affairs would continue...

As he watched, Ryan realized that the shimmering rainbow glow around Nechronus was fading, flickering out. The light died, Nechronus slumped, and the robe collapsed. The mask fell to the floor with a clatter while the robe sagged into the chair like so much drapery. It was only too obvious that there hadn't been anything inside of it while it was getting some sort of magical recharging.

Ryan's mind raced frantically as he tried to figure it out. Had there ever been anything solid inside the robe, or was Nechronus just some sort of mind without a physical body? And if so, did that mean Nechronus was dead now and they didn't have anything more to worry about?

"Just who are you?"

Ryan whirled. It was the fat kid who had spoken. No longer disoriented and confused, he was alert and fully conscious, glaring at him, standing erect and confident, strangely imposing even as a grossly obese boy in his skivvies. There was something cold in the now arrogant face, contorted with fury though it was. Then the truth dawned on Ryan. His guess about what purpose the boy served had been completely wrong.

He wasn't just a boy.

He was Nechronus.

Outside of his robe and mask, he was still a boy, a boy who had stayed a boy for centuries by magical means. Like Peter Pan, only meaner. A lot meaner.

For a second, Ryan almost thought he knew him. There had been a boy like this back at his old school, spoiled, selfish, bullying, cruel. Even allowing for some kind of loop in time, it would have been too much of a coincidence for that boy to have turned out to be Nechronus himself, but given the power to indulge his every whim and make everyone do what he wanted, he probably would have ended up just like him. It was Nechronus's luck that he could do what the kid Ryan had known could only dream of.

Nechronus didn't wait for an answer to his question. Perhaps he was past caring who Ryan was, seeing him only as someone who for no reason that could possibly matter had interrupted this supremely important bodily renewal process.

"How dare you even think of laying your filthy hands on me!" he exclaimed in an oddly high voice, the voice of a fourteen-year-old boy instead of the mighty magician he was supposed to be. He raised a hand—

And Ryan was knocked backwards by an invisible wave of pure force into a bank of machinery. The back of his head struck something hard and stars danced in front of his eyes for a moment. He slumped to the floor, his strength suddenly gone. The wave hadn't even been precisely aimed. He had only been clipped by the edge of it, which was bad enough. Being hit full on...

Through the pain and disorientation, he realized that he was done for. His truncheon, the only weapon he had, was gone, dropped or stripped out of his hand. He couldn't run, and even if he could there was nowhere to run. Nechronus could blast him before he could get very far in any direction.

"Master!"

Startled by the voice, Nechronus held off on delivering the killing blow and lowered his arm. "What is it?"

A slim, blond boy wearing a red-jacketed drum major uniform ran into the pool of light on the stage. He came to an abrupt stop in front of the throne where the empty robe lay, and looked around frantically until he saw the fat boy.

"Master!" he gasped, out of breath. "The servants are rebelling! They're overrunning the guards, they've even killed several Antroids—"

"Then what are you doing here, you incompetent dolt?" Nechronus roared, and the officer cringed in the face of such pure anger. "Concentrate the human guards, make a stand, and kill as many servants as you need to! Those we can always replace, but the Antroid queen will make trouble if we lose too many of her mercenaries! Now go back out there and put the revolt down! Must I remind you how close you are to needing your youth renewed, and what will happen if it isn't?"

The officer turned pale and gulped. "Yes, Master! But what about you? You're out of your robe! If you don't get back into it soon—"

"I am fully aware of that, lackey, and I shall attend to that matter! At least once I've absorbed the powers of these two magicians, I won't have to spend half my life wrapped up in the thrice-cursed thing. But first, we must restore order so we can then continue the process. Before you go, however, eliminate this petty nuisance." He waved a casually dismissive hand in the direction of Ryan, huddled by the base of the machinery and still too dazed to stand.

The officer stiffened and saluted. "Yes, Master!"

Without even a backwards glance, Nechronus turned and started towards the throne where his robe lay, on the other side of the lab. He moved slowly and heavily, as though walking was difficult for him outside of his robe. Too little exercise over the years, perhaps...

The officer faced Ryan and thumbed his truncheon on. If the things had a default setting, it was probably low-intensity to avoid accidents. But apparently they could be adjusted in some way Ryan hadn't figured out yet, and it was obvious from the lurid red sparks the truncheon was emitting with a loud crackle that this wasn't just a phaser set to "stun."

Ryan was recovering fast, but all his clearing senses told him was that he was in bad trouble with no way to escape and perhaps only seconds left to live. The officer was aiming the truncheon at him, the blazing red sparks between the electrodes were building, he was about to fire—

Suddenly a shimmering blue wall flared up just inches in front of Ryan's nose. The scarlet discharge from the truncheon hit the shield in a burst of brilliant fireworks but scattered harmlessly.

Half-blinded from the sudden glare, Ryan blinked and glanced to his right. Bill crouched there, holding up his truncheon and projecting the protective force shield against the officer's attack.

He grinned at Ryan. "Gotcha covered! Now go stop Laughing Boy while I take care of this goon!"

Ryan nodded gratefully, thinking that saving his life was just like something a dad would do. But he still had no idea how he could stop Nechronus without being flattened again, or worse.

"Keep him from putting that robe back on," Bill added through clenched teeth as he held the truncheon and its protective shield against the officer's attack. "Talitha thinks he gets his power from it, and maybe we can hold him up until Karlo comes to. Now move!"

For a moment, Ryan thought he heard his father talking with those last two words. He threw himself to one side, out of the shield. The guard started to turn towards him with his leveled truncheon, but Bill rose to intercept. What followed was a confused fight between equally matched opponents, both armed with truncheons that projected protective shields of pure force, each stalking the other warily while looking for a weak spot.

Ryan was too intent on getting to Nechronus to watch the duel very closely, but as he worked his way along in back of the control board, he saw Bill and the guard out the corner of his eye engaging in a burst of blue shields and lurid red lightning. It was a test of strength, the irresistible force of the truncheons versus the immovable objects of the shields, then both truncheons were abruptly torn out of their hands by the impact when they met head-on and went flying off to the side.

That gave Bill his opening and he dove at the officer in a flurry of fists. Both went down and they rolled on the floor exchanging blows where they could. Ryan hadn't known his father had been such a tough scrapper. Probably not wanting his son to get any wrong ideas, Mr. Thayer had never mentioned anything about the occasional playground scuffle.

There was no time to stand by and cheer him on. Even though Nechronus was barely able to walk on his own, he had almost reached the throne where his robe lay. Amazed that he was actually doing this, Ryan ran forward and leaped at Nechronus from the rear. With one arm wrapped around his fleshy neck, he tried to pull the massive body down. Having to embrace all that flabby, moist flesh was not the most pleasant thing Ryan had ever done.

Even though Nechronus outweighed him by a considerable amount, Ryan had caught him by surprise, off-balance and in mid-stride, and at too close a range for him to use his magical defenses effectively. Nechronus buckled at the knees and went sprawling forward, hitting the floor heavily with a loud splat of sweat-slick flesh and a choked gurgle.

Ryan hit the floor as well and tried to roll out of Nechronus's reach as fast as he could. There was about to be one very angry master magician looking for somebody to hurt, and Ryan wasn't sure slowing him down for a few seconds had accomplished anything.

No, actually it had. It had given Talitha time to run out of the shadows and to the throne. She scooped the helmet off the floor and tossed it into the surrounding darkness, then pulled the robe free from the throne. It didn't come easily, as it had been attached to the seat by tubes and wires that she had to pop out. In the process, she uncovered a pair of boots with six-inch soles and some kind of stilt-like leg bracing. For good measure, Talitha kicked them away.

Struggling clumsily and ponderously to his feet and seeing what Talitha had done, Nechronus was aghast, and suddenly forgot all about Ryan.

"No-o-o-o!"

He hurled a bolt of sizzling electricity at Talitha but she dodged it, dropping the robe on the floor and diving behind the control console. In turn, while Nechronus's attention was directed at Talitha, Ryan had the few seconds he needed to duck in back of one of the tables. How safe he would be if Nechronus really got worked up, he wasn't sure, but at least it was something for the moment.

Nechronus reached for the robe. "No one dares touch me!" he raged. "I don't know who you people are but none of you will live to see another day! None of you!"

He was interrupted by an altercation at the entrance to the amphitheater, past the outermost ring of seats: a loud bang as the doors burst open, shouting, screams. A crowd of people poured in, pursuing some last few bug guards and their even fewer human officers amid shouts of "Down with Nechronus!"

Leaving the crumpled robe aside, Nechronus staggered to the edge of the stage and raised his arms.

"Enough!" he shouted in a voice that seemed far too loud to have come out of a human throat.

Everyone in the place stopped at once and looked up fearfully. Even if most of his servants had never seen him outside of his robe, they knew only too well from the booming voice who the fat boy had to be.

"Are you mad?" Nechronus thundered. "Have you no idea what would happen if I am overthrown? Only I can keep you young! Without me, you would all get old!"

There was a pause, then a voice that sounded like Thomas's called out, "Better to get old than serve you as a slave!" To the crowd: "Without his robe of power, even the mighty Lord Nechronus is naught but a boy! We can bring him down!"

The crowd roared in approval and Nechronus must have realized that he had lost the argument. His rule, even his life, were now dependent on what he did next.

He reared up in all his fury, raising his suddenly glowing arms as though to gather all his magical potential and strike with the force of a hundred lightning bolts at once.

"You fools!" he shrieked. "The robe only keeps me from aging! My true power has always been within me! You are no different from those who mocked me so long ago! Now I shall destroy all of *you* just as I destroyed all of *them!*"

Eyes clenched shut, Ryan waited for the inevitable firestorm that would rain down. *This is it*, he thought bleakly. *We lost.* After being knocked around and humiliated for the first time in centuries, and now facing open revolt from his subjects, Nechronus was mad enough that he would probably kill everybody in the place, friend and enemy both, and start over with fresh slaves.

Seconds ticked by. Somehow, something didn't seem right. Something that should have been happening wasn't happening.

What's taking him so long? Amazed that he wasn't dead already, Ryan opened one eye warily.

Something *had* happened — to Nechronus. His body stood rigid, frozen in the attacking pose, but his eyes were wide in utter terror, not focused on anything he was seeing, but looking as though he had realized something inside of himself had gone terribly wrong.

As Ryan stared, Nechronus's bloated boyish features seemed to blur, even melt. Wrinkles appeared on his face, hair turned white and fell away. Too long out of his life-sustaining robe and away from the rejuvenating bath of rainbow colors, he was reverting to what his true form should have been. Just how old was he by this time, anyway?

Then the inevitable consequence of a normal lifetime's worth of aging concentrated within a couple of minutes hit him.

Nechronus crumpled to the floor, dried up, shriveled — and died.

For a few moments, the entire amphitheater was eerily silent.

Even Bill and the officer, who had still been fighting, broke off to stare in amazement. Then the officer ran to the front of the stage.

"The Master is dead!" he shouted to the crowd. "Now I am the new Master! Bow down before me—"

He was suddenly engulfed in a blaze of crackling blue electricity. He managed a brief scream before collapsing. The lightning faded away, leaving him lying on the floor gasping, his arms and legs still twitching.

"That will be quite enough of that."

Karlo stepped into the spotlight while leaning on Talitha, holding his wand up. It must have been taken from him when he was captured but somehow he had it back. He still looked a little worse for wear, but even weakened and limping, he radiated power and authority. He turned to face the crowd out in the amphitheater.

"Nechronus is indeed dead," he proclaimed in a voice that sounded tired and yet carried to the far walls, "but there will be no new Master. You are now all free!"

The vast room erupted in cheers.

With his back against the table, Ryan sagged in relief. It had been a long day, and now it was over...

Chapter Ten

Somewhere far away, he heard Bill's voice. "Hey, wake up!" Then somebody very close by had grabbed his shoulder and was shaking him. "We're going home soon, unless you want to stay here!"

Blearily, Ryan opened his eyes and saw Bill looking down at him, smiling despite the black eye and some dried blood under his nose.

"What's going on?" Ryan asked, trying to shake the fog out of his head.

"Karlo's been cleaning up the mess, basically," Bill said. "This castle's like a whole little town, and we just knocked off the guy who was running it. So he had to figure out who to leave in charge and keep things going until he can come back. He's just about done with that, though, and then we can pack up and pull out!"

As Ryan got to his feet, he saw that the amphitheater was empty and he and Bill were the only ones on the stage. No, they weren't quite alone. Nechronus still lay where he had fallen. Somebody had thrown a sheet over him, but no one had gotten up the nerve to remove the body. Even dead, Nechronus probably still terrified those who'd had to serve him for so long.

Moments later, Karlo and Talitha appeared from out of the shadows and joined them.

"I appointed your friend Thomas as provisional Lord of the Castle," Karlo told Bill and Ryan. "Since he was capable enough to lead the uprising, he seemed the logical choice. I promised to return as soon as possible to address the unfinished business. We shall have to send all the children whence they came, where they can resume their old lives and age normally. If they wish to go, that is. Many came from circumstances to which they have no desire to return, such as orphans, homeless on the streets, even outright slavery, as was the case with the African-descended lad from

Louisiana in 1840. For some of them, life in servitude to Nechronus was actually preferable to what they had known before and we would do them no favors sending them back."

Nor was that the only headache, Karlo added. Nechronus had also been a power on some sort of magicians' council. While his sudden removal from the scene would mainly cause everyone to react with a sigh of relief, there were also consequences that would reverberate far beyond just the castle walls.

"If only you three knew the magnitude of what you've done," Karlo said with a weary sigh. "Fortunately for your peace of mind, your duty is done. All that is left is to take you home as soon as Gadwell Thayer returns." He glanced at the shrouded remnant of what had been Nechronus and nodded thoughtfully. "Now I understand why I was so insistent that all three of you accompany me. Left to myself, I would have been content to spirit the prisoners away and avoid a direct confrontation with Nechronus himself, since as events proved anyway it would have been a battle I could not win. You three, however, even with no magical ability at all, managed to destroy him on your own."

"Er... not exactly," Ryan was quick to make clear. "It's more like we just kept him busy and out of his robe until his inner rot thing caught up with him. A minute or two more and we would have been toast. Literally."

"Nonetheless," Karlo said, "the fact remains that he is dead and you are alive. It speaks well of you however it happened. Even armed with genuine magical powers, it is only in fairy stories that an inexperienced boy magician could battle an evil master mage centuries old and emerge victorious. It is more likely such a callow youth would be crushed like an insect in the first few pages."

Maybe Bill had the best take on it as he stared curiously down at Nechronus's remains. "I guess," he said, "we all have to grow up sometime. This is what happens if you don't."

Gadwell finally showed up about then. He had been busy with dismissing the surviving bug-warriors and arranging for their return to their hive. Just the thought that there were monsters like that here made Ryan wonder what other strange marvels this magical world might hold. Unfortunately, he would probably never know.

Gadwell effusively thanked Ryan, Bill, and Talitha for rescuing him and everybody else, and shook their hands. "You kids really do have the Thayer stuff in you!" he exclaimed delightedly. It would have been fine if he had left it at that, but he went on to say, "Now that the menace of Nechronus has been eliminated, I can safely have another Christmas party next year!"

It would be nice to see Bill and Talitha again, Ryan thought, but he certainly didn't want to go through anything like this again.

Gadwell must have read his expression. "No, I think you've had your turn, but your brother might be about old enough by then!"

Karlo abruptly spoke up. "I wish to have a few words with you, Gadwell Thayer."

Even though Uncle Gadwell was a fairly old man, Ryan recognized his expression. He had seen it on the faces of his friends when an irate teacher caught them doing something they shouldn't and told them to report to the Principal's office — *now*.

Arms akimbo, Karlo stood in front of Gadwell and looked him in the eye. Gadwell tried to turn his head away from the accusing glare but apparently couldn't make his body obey his brain's desperate orders.

"What in the name of Thaumaturgy," Karlo rumbled, "gave you the mad notion of having a party for children from different eras in the first place, with all the potential for catastrophically disrupting the orderly flow of time with paradoxes beyond calculation, and in a place dangerously exposed to any dark mage who caught wind of it?"

The amazing thing for Ryan was that at this stage in their respective lives, Gadwell was actually older than Karlo, yet Gadwell deferred to him like a teenage boy trying to explain the new dent in the family car to his father.

"I'm sorry, Master! It just seemed like a pleasant thing to do for the children of various generations in my family and some of their neighborhood friends, and I was curious to see how children of different eras would react to one another. I was well aware of the danger, of course, and although it was something I had long wanted to do, I never dared before now. This year, however, I looked into the future and saw indications that Nechronus had died about this time, so I felt safe in going ahead with it."

Karlo closed his eyes and touched his fingertips to his forehead, as though to contemplate what he had just heard with the appropriate display of exasperation.

"It might have been wise to ascertain exactly *when* Nechronus died before giving your party," he said, "but now it appears that the party itself set the events in motion that led to his long overdue demise. Perhaps you are more to be pitied than censured as just one more fly caught in the spider web of Fate... But what is this matter of addressing me as 'Master'? I've not even met you yet! When we do meet, and apparently I am destined to take you on as my apprentice whether I care to or not, I should warn you against any harebrained notions such as holding trans-temporal Christmas parties. Now that you've done it anyway, I shall have to bite my tongue and let you do it!" He sighed and turned to the others. "Enough of this. The time has come to return you three to your proper time and place."

"Yeah, let's blow this pop stand!" Bill exclaimed.

"I won't even ask what that means…" Karlo muttered and lifted his wand.

They rematerialized in the hallway with the doors. Mrs. Gadwell and the rest of the kids were waiting for them, sitting on the floor along the walls. From the sound of things, they had been waiting there for hours, just as long in their time as Ryan had been in the magical world, and they had never been entirely certain anyone would ever come to collect them. Their relief in seeing the two magicians appear was all but overwhelming, though the tough '30s kid just grumbled, "What took ya so long?"

Bill looked at Ryan. "Do you want to slug him or can I get first crack?"

Ryan could tell that Bill wasn't more than half-serious about the idea, satisfying though it might have been, and just shook his head.

While Gadwell went to work on the long and tedious process of sending his other party guests home, Karlo had Ryan, Bill, and Talitha follow him into the party room. There, they stood in front of the door that led out into the basement.

Karlo waved his wand at the door to set up some sort of magical field, a process that took a few minutes since he had to get the timing just right. It would be more than embarrassing if Ryan and the others were returned to their own eras but, say, two minutes before they left and ran into themselves when they hadn't before. Meanwhile, it sank in on the three that it was finally goodbye.

"Aw, c'mon!" Bill exclaimed. "Why so sad? It isn't like we won't see each other again."

Ryan realized that he had been thinking of them as simply Bill and Talitha for a while now, and not as his father and daughter. Whatever their more technical relationship was, here they had been friends his own age. He also realized that he was going to miss them.

"Yeah, but it won't be like this."

"Guess you got a point," Bill said. "The next time I see you, I'll be changing your diapers."

Ryan winced, then glanced at Talitha. "And the same goes for—"

"You don't have to say it," she said, her face turning almost as red as her jumpsuit.

Karlo had now finished his incantations. He opened the door, revealing the dark and dusty old basement, and cleared his throat. "I cannot delay this any longer. You may go first, William, since this is your time."

Talitha hugged Bill. "You're going to be a wonderful grandpa!"

"Maybe so," Bill said, "but let's not rush it. I'll probably spoil you rotten, though…"

Hey, how about spoiling your son first? Ryan thought. Then, when Talitha was done hugging — girls did that a lot — he shook hands with Bill. They grinned at each other, but there didn't seem to be anything more that needed saying. It was a guy thing.

"See you in a few." Bill started to turn towards the doorway.

"Just a moment, please," Karlo said.

"Say wha'?" Bill asked, pausing to look back at him.

Karlo stepped up, pressed the palm of his right hand firmly against Bill's forehead, and chanted something dark and mysterious. Bill staggered back, his eyes suddenly looking glazed. Karlo took hold of his shoulder, turned him back towards the doorway, and gave him a gentle shove. Bill shuffled unsteadily on through and Karlo closed the door after him.

"What did you do to him?" Ryan demanded in alarm.

"There is no need to be concerned," Karlo assured him with professional detachment. "It was merely a trifling adjustment of his cerebral cortex. It would not do for him to know too much about his own future."

"I don't see why not," Ryan started to say, then stopped short. His father had forgotten what had happened to his younger self, so having his memory erased was necessary for events to play out the way they should — or had. But was it really necessary for *him*?

Karlo pointed his wand at the door again and incanted another spell, then opened it. The scene outside had changed. No longer the dark, dingy basement, it was now clean and brightly lit. Two people were standing just outside the doorway, as though waiting, but they were somewhat silhouetted by the light and it was hard to make them out.

Karlo nodded to Talitha. "It is now time for you to go, too."

"Wait a sec." Talitha hugged Ryan and kissed his cheek. "Just be a little nicer to Mom, okay?"

Ryan was about to say something about "Mom" having to be nice to him first, but decided this wasn't the time or place to argue about it. He just promised, "You can depend on it."

"I *am* depending on it!" Talitha exclaimed.

As he disengaged from the hug, Ryan could now see the people waiting for Talitha on the other side of the doorway more clearly and it dawned on him who they had to be. With a start, he briefly glimpsed himself as he would be in — what? his mid-40s? — but it was Kelsey who caught his eye. The years would be very good to her. Ryan had a sense that he had underestimated what the bratty girl who sat next to him in school would one day become. She saw him through the doorway and smiled warmly, making him feel somewhere beyond strange.

Karlo approached Talitha with an outstretched hand. "But first—"

"I don't think so!" Talitha adroitly ducked under his arm and hopped through the doorway. As soon as she was clear and falling into her parents' welcoming arms, her world dissolved into gray fog. Karlo shut the door after her and that was the last Ryan would see of her for something like fifteen years. Even then it would be a while before she was much good for conversation.

Now it was Ryan's turn. Karlo opened the door once more, and the basement of his time appeared, dark and dirty just as it had been in Bill's time. Then Karlo turned and faced him, standing in the doorway as though making sure Ryan wouldn't be able to dodge him the way Talitha had, and lifted his hand, palm out.

"Wait!" Ryan exclaimed, realizing that he didn't want to forget what had happened and thinking fast. He remembered what Karlo himself had said to Uncle Gadwell, that he couldn't stop Gadwell from having the ill-advised Christmas party because he had already gone and done it. "You saw me and my future wife just now. We were waiting for Talitha. That means we must have known what had happened to her, which also means I didn't forget about all this, and that means you never messed with my brain in the first place. So you can't do it because you never did it!"

"I—" Karlo began, but didn't get any further, still trying to think it through. He looked at his palm, then at Ryan, and threw up his arms in hopeless resignation. "I suppose it does spare me the trouble of having to cleanse the minds of your family as well. But you may find that you would prefer to forget what you have just learned and experienced. Now be off with you!"

Ryan stepped through the doorway — and was home.

Epilogue

As soon as he got back, Ryan had to debrief his family about what he had been through.

"I did all that?" his father said in utter amazement. "And now I don't even remember any of it!" He added a rather pungent opinion about Karlo under his breath that shocked Ryan, since he had never heard him use that word before.

His mother was just plain horrified when he told the story and declared that if she had known even half of what was going to happen, she never would have agreed to let him go. Grandpa's insistence that Ryan had had to go whether she liked it or not just led to a stormy family argument without really settling anything.

Ryan tried to have a private conversation with his father about it all later, but it was hardly satisfying. He really wanted to talk to Bill, who was twenty-five years in the past. While his father may have once been a breezy, wisecracking teenager, he had grown up, decided to use his native intelligence for something other than figuring batting averages, and concentrated on making a living and supporting a family. Now he wasn't a buddy Ryan could confide in, but just another grown-up, and one who could tell him to go out and shovel the snow and he would have to do it. Even more depressing was realizing that thirty years down the road, Talitha was probably experiencing the same feeling of disconnect with *her* father…

After that, it was a quiet few days until Christmas, and Ryan felt he could do without any more excitement for a while. Reading about dauntless heroes having adventures in books was all very well, but actually having an adventure was something else. He had been too close to death too many times to appreciate the adrenaline rush. The magic ring that had taken him to 1895 was now just an inert piece of metal and tucked away in a drawer as a souvenir to remind him now and then that the adventure had really happened, and that was where he preferred to leave it.

He just wondered what he would say to Kelsey when he saw her again back at school.

As Ryan had expected, Christmas morning was a bit of a disappointment for his younger brother and sister. The family finances just couldn't stretch for many or very expensive presents. Being older and more aware of how things were, Ryan was able to accept it. He'd seen a mall Santa interviewed on TV saying he knew times were hard when kids actually asked him for a new pair of socks, and that was very nearly the case in this house.

The family was gathered in the living room, with the grown-ups in the chairs and on the couch, and the kids on the floor surrounded by empty boxes and torn holiday wrapping paper. Even a hard-times Christmas morning with just a few presents had left its share of clutter. It was the late Christmas morning lull, with all the presents opened but dinner wouldn't be for a while yet, and no one wanted to do much. Even the conversation dragged a bit, until it turned to where they would all be next Christmas.

Ryan's mother shook her head. "It's a beautiful house and I love living here... but it just bothers me knowing that... *room* is right under us. How can I sleep at night worrying about what might come out of it?"

"Uncle Gadwell's laboratory?" Grandpa asked with a laugh. "Nothing to worry about. It's just an empty and dusty old room now, locked up good and tight."

"Well, if you say so..." Mrs. Thayer said a little doubtfully.

That was when they heard it. Distant, muffled footsteps, as though someone was coming up the basement stairs. Then there was a knock on the other side of the closed basement door in the kitchen.

Everyone looked at each other with wide eyes, then at Grandpa.

"I think," Grandpa said slowly, "somebody ought to answer that..."

"I'll go," Mr. Thayer said, and got up from his chair.

"Be careful, dear!" Mrs. Thayer called worriedly after him.

"If our mysterious caller is polite enough to knock," Grandpa said none too confidently, "there shouldn't be too much to worry about."

It was Uncle Gadwell, dressed for the 1890s in his suit, tie, and vest, and with his arms full of presents.

"There were gifts for everyone at the party," he explained, "but we were interrupted and Ryan never got his. So I thought I'd deliver it myself, and while I was about it, I brought a few things for the rest of you."

With that, some more Christmas cheer came to 128 West Fairground

Street than anticipated.

Ryan's little sister got a doll. A very high-tech, walking, talking doll about two and a half feet tall, resembling a miniature ten-year-old in rather futuristic clothes that resembled overalls.

"Will you be my fwend?" the doll lisped.

The doll seemed to have something of a mind of its own and spent a lot of its time watching TV with apparent interest. Ryan wondered if it had originally been Talitha's, the doll she said hadn't been getting along with the cat.

For Ryan's brother, Uncle Gadwell brought a road-racing set from circa 1963 called Aurora Model Motoring with HO-scale cars.

"A little after my time," Gadwell admitted, "but it somehow survived the battle in Nechronus's play room and turned up when we were cleaning out the castle. I heard one of my fellow wizards speak highly of it as a cherished boyhood memory, and I thought Cody might enjoy it as well."

Cody seemed dubious at first, since it was so retro, but finally decided that after such a sparse Christmas he'd better be happy with what he got and maybe the road-racing set had some play potential after all.

Ryan could tell that his elaborately wrapped present was a book even before he opened it, but the surprise was what the book was. It was a thick, sumptuously bound and illustrated 19th Century book in perfect, like new condition. He had every reason to suspect it *was* brand new. The title was *Vingt mille lieues sous les mers* par Jules Verne.

Ryan wasn't sure whether to be delighted or dismayed. It was obviously *Twenty Thousand Leagues Under the Sea* from the numerous engraved black and white illustrations of undersea scenes, but...

"It, er, seems to be in French," he said.

"All the more incentive to learn, I dare say," Uncle Gadwell replied breezily. "In the meantime, I suggest that you inspect the fly leaf."

Ryan wasn't sure what a "fly leaf" was but opened the front cover anyway and saw a scribble on the first page. "Somebody wrote on it. Oh — it's autographed."

Ryan could only imagine how Uncle Gadwell had arranged *that*.

It took some puzzling with his French dictionary later, but Ryan eventually translated the accompanying inscription.

"To my good friend Ryan, whom I will never know, but who will read this book over a hundred years after I am gone in a world of unimaginable wonders that I wish I could live to see."

It was probably safe to say that none of the other guys at Centerpoint High had a copy of a Jules Verne novel personally inscribed to them by the author, but the thrill was diminished somewhat by the fact that none of them would believe he had one even if he showed it to them since he couldn't prove how he had come by it. This would go on the bookshelf as a matter of quiet pride and his own satisfaction. Maybe someday he might even be able to read it, though from glancing through it he got the idea that a lot of the book was just lists of fish in the world's oceans as seen through the submarine viewing port.

After presents for the rest of the family were passed out, Uncle Gadwell was about to go back to wherever he had come from, but Ryan's mother suggested that he stay for dinner. He gladly accepted the invitation, and while having a wizard from 1900 or so as a guest was a little intimidating at first, he was personable and good-humored enough to soon put everyone else at their ease. Ryan had to admit that it certainly made the meal more lively when one of the diners had the power of levitation.

"Would someone please pass the butter?" Uncle Gadwell asked a little theatrically. "Never mind, I'll get it myself." He made a pass with his hand and the dish with the butter on it rose from the table and floated towards him.

Show-off! Ryan thought.

After dessert, Uncle Gadwell stood up from the table. "Now I really must take my leave. Thank you for the lovely dinner. There is nothing better than spending Christmas with one's family, even if it's family I mostly hadn't met yet. I wish you one and all a very merry Christmas!"

Everyone said their good-byes and thank yous for the presents, and he strode off to the kitchen. The last they heard of him was his fading steps going down the basement steps.

For a few moments, no one seemed certain what to say, then Ryan broke the silence by commenting,

"Next Christmas is going to seem pretty dull after this one."

"Let's *hope* so," his mother said fervently.

Just as everyone was starting to make tentative movements in the direction of getting up from the table, Mr. Thayer stood up to make an announcement.

"There just aren't any job openings out there," he said. "At least not doing what I was doing. But sending out all those resumes got some results I didn't expect — several offers for free-lance consulting work. Maybe a permanent full-time job with benefits is too much to hope for these days, but if I can build up my own business as a free-lancer and consultant... We might as well unpack all the boxes and settle in for good. We won't have to move away from Centerpoint after all."

"You can live here as long as you like," Grandma put in. "We'd hate to leave this house after all these years, but it's too big for just the two of us. With you folks here, we won't have to keep it up by ourselves or move someplace smaller."

Ryan had a strange feeling of Destiny closing in on him. Now it looked as though he would be going to school with Kelsey for years to come instead of making his escape at the end of this year. Perhaps it was just as well, since there wouldn't be any Talitha otherwise, but he'd still like to feel that he had some choice in the matter. He remembered the glimpse he'd had of Kelsey's grown-up self, though, and he could see how in the end he would fall in love with her of his own free will.

Free will?

Was there such a thing?

Somewhere in the back of his mind, he thought he could hear Uncle Gadwell laughing.

A Hard Day's Flight

Introduction

"A Hard Day's Flight" was written around 1999/2000 as part of a series of stories based on the premise that my most beloved childhood fantasy — being able to fly like Superman — had actually come true when I was of an age to have some fun with it. While intended as a standalone story that could be understood without having to read what had gone before, "Flight" was about the sixth or seventh installment in the run.

Most of the previous stories have been consolidated into a novel and published under the title *A Dream Flying*. "A Hard Day's Flight" takes place a month or so after the events of the novel and has not been published before (except in a low-circulation fanzine that hardly anyone ever saw circa 2000). Since it has a Christmas theme, it sees print here as a bonus.

The backstory is that Kyle Rhodebeck (nicknamed Sparky), a fifteen-year-old paperboy in the small town of New Romford, Ohio, stumbled across a long-buried alien spaceship in the summer of 1967. The not quite intentional result of that close encounter of the weird kind was the implantation of a small device in his chest that gave him the power to fly.

Realizing that going public with it would likely change his life more drastically than he would like, Kyle has tried to keep his flying ability a secret, not only from his parents but from his friends and even girls he likes a lot. He has been seen from a distance on occasion, however, giving rise to a local legend of a "Mystery Bird."

Shortly after school started in September, his classmate Janet Larsen accidentally discovered that he had this flying thing going on. So far, she is the only other person who knows his secret, and their relationship is about that of an ambitious big sister and her somewhat dim little brother. Janet is a hyper-competent doer, in all the clubs and active in everything, while Kyle is a bookish hermit who has enough trouble keeping his paper route afloat. Since Janet can do anything except fly, and that's the one thing Kyle *can* do, he is always being pulled into her schemes even when he would rather stay home and read comic books and sci-fi paperbacks.

As recounted in *A Dream Flying*, one of Janet's recent bright ideas had Kyle stuffed into the school mascot costume so he could fly at the Homecoming football game with no one knowing it was him or how he was doing it. The aftershocks from that little episode are still reverberating as "A Hard Day's Flight" begins.

A Hard Day's Flight

Or, How Sparky Saved Christmas

Maybe someday, hundreds of years from now, everyone will be able to fly like Superman. But in the fall of 1967, it was just me, a fifteen-year-old kid named Kyle Rhodebeck, thanks to the long-ago landing of an alien spaceship in the middle of Ohio.

I had some misgivings about the use I was getting out of my new-found power, though.

Thursday, November 16, 1967

Just as I was coming home from school that afternoon, a stray dog wandered into our yard and spotted the cat arching and stretching on the front porch. The dog barked and took off for the cat. Tippy screeched and bolted in an orange and white-striped blur. With the dog right behind, the cat leaped off the far end of the porch and hit the ground running. Tippy headed straight for the maple tree in the right front corner of the yard and scrabbled up the trunk. Frustrated, the dog stood on its hind legs at the base of the tree, front paws against the trunk, and barked up at the cat rapidly climbing through the leafless branches.

At this point, I decided to take a hand. I trotted towards the tree and yelled, "Beat it, Bowser!"

The dog glanced at me, startled. Maybe it sensed something, since the flying unit embedded in my chest did generate an invisible energy field that an animal might be able to pick up on. Or maybe my sudden arrival on the scene just scared it. Whatever the reason, it promptly forgot about Tippy, dropped back down to four legs, and skedaddled across the Rogers's front yard next door and on to parts unknown.

That left me with one cat up one tree. Now, it's true that cats can get down from trees. As smart-alecks like to point out, you don't see too many skeletons of cats that starved to death up in the branches. It's just that the lovable furballs never seem to remember from one time to the next how they got down before, and have to figure it out all over again. Rather than wait for Tippy to get that walnut-sized kitty brain of his working on the problem (and mainly so I could feed him before I started on my paper route), I decided to go up after him.

Of the four trees we had on the property, that particular maple was the best one for climbing. The trunk forked just a few feet above the ground, unlike the other trees whose lowest branches were way out of reach. Of course, now that I had the power to fly, it hardly mattered, but I had to keep it believable in case anybody was watching (like Mrs. Rogers at her kitchen window), so I pretended to shinny up the trunk. The fact that it was known to be a good climbing tree even before ol' Sparky went air-borne and Mrs. Rogers had seen me climb it for real any number of times over the years would cover for how effortlessly I actually clambered up into the branches.

I found Tippy crouched on a horizontal limb, breathing hard and fur fluffed, as though warily watching in case the dog came back. After having a cat for eight years, one thing I had learned the hard way was not to try to pick up an agitated feline too abruptly. So I took it easy and spoke softly and soothingly as I crawled out on the branch towards him.

Tippy calmed down fairly quickly. Being chased up a tree by a dog was probably all in a day's work for a cat, and since he had never been in any serious danger, he wasn't any more upset than he had to be. In a moment or two he was letting me stroke his back. Still, his eye was on where he had last seen the dog, and he hardly even seemed to notice my petting.

After another few moments, he had gotten over his fright and I was able to gather him up in my arms without him shredding the bark trying to hold onto the branch (or shredding me). I can't claim to understand how a cat thinks, but he knew he had to get down somehow, and based on past experience he may have figured it would be a lot easier if he just let me take care of it. I half-stood on the branch, braced against the trunk with my shoulder. My thought was to simulate shinnying down for the sake of credibility, even if both my arms were full of cat at the moment.

About then, my mother came out the front door of the house onto the porch. She looked around, then saw me up in the tree with Tippy.

"Sparky?" she called, using the Dreaded Nickname. "I thought I heard a racket out here. What's going on?"

"Dog chased Tippy up the tree," I replied. "Just thought I'd go after him."

"Well, just be careful getting down," Mom said. "You might fall." Then she turned around and went back into the house.

"*You might fall,*" I muttered to myself and to the tomcat in my arms. Mom meant well, of course, but for some reason that admonishment stuck in my craw. To heck with credibility. Nobody was probably watching anyway. I hopped off the branch and into space. It was a fall under power, braked the whole way down, taken slowly and easily, not even scaring the cat in my arms, and he usually didn't like flying with me. I touched down on the ground with hardly even a jar. It was a petty act of defiance, but sometimes I just got so tired of having to keep my flying power a secret...

Even so, I thought as I bent to put Tippy on the ground, there had to be a more important way to use the power to fly than just getting cats down from trees.

Monday, November 20

When does the Christmas season start?

That depends on who you ask. My parents would say, "earlier every year." (And they said *that* every year.)

If you wanted to nail it down a little closer, my answer would be, "Right after Labor Day." That was when the Sears Christmas catalog, commonly known as "The Wishbook," hit the mailbox at 112 Parrott Street. In my younger days, the arrival of that thick tome was what sent visions of electric trains and Marx playsets dancing through my head, and ignited months of dreaming and scheming.

But while that may have been the beginning of the season for a greedy little kid, school was just starting and we still had Halloween and Thanksgiving to get through. Christmas didn't really pop up on the horizon ahead until the smell of roasting turkey was in the air.

I finally pinpointed the starting gun as going off on Thanksgiving morning, when Captain Kangaroo and Mr. Greenjeans hosted the TV coverage of the various parades around the country with all the big balloons. After the parades were over, Santa Claus showed up in the TV studio and he and Captain K. and Mr. G. sat down at a table for a traditional turkey dinner with all the trimmings. That was the moment. Roll the credits and we're on our way. Next stop, December 25.

That was my personal little notion of it, anyway. The merchants of New Romford had their own ideas.

"How did you get roped into this?" I asked Janet Larsen in Study Hall.

"Simple," Janet said. "The shopping center people wanted Freddy Falcon to help Santa pass out toys to the kids. You may not realize it, but ever since Freddy flew at the Homecoming game, he's gotten really

95

NEW ROMFORD, OH., HIGH SCHOOL

popular with the little kids. He's right up there with Santa Claus now, so they thought the two of them together would be a winner."

It was Fourth Period "Honor Study Hall," called that because it was unsupervised. It was just a dozen of us kids who had come up extra without any other place to go that period when somebody in the Front Office worked out the class assignments, so we were shoved into a third-floor classroom off in a remote corner of the old part of the high school, with Janet appointed room monitor to make sure nobody broke the windows or got into fistfights. Some kids talked quietly among themselves, one or two stared out the window at barren tree branches black and stark against a grey sky, and a few actually tried to study.

Janet and I sat next to each other in the back of the room and I usually spent the first few minutes of the period talking to her. Besides being awfly purdy with her stylishly coifed dark hair, she was smart and got some of the top grades in the school. Though there were some odd rumors floating around school because we had been seen together so much lately, we weren't a Couple or anything like that. I was a booky hermit by nature, just a goofy kid with glasses and nothing much to look at, and completely out of things socially, while Janet was right in the middle of the social scene and making it all happen. It was just that she was the only person who knew I could fly.

Anybody else with her schedule chock full of after-school Activities would have looked at an open spot on Wednesday afternoon with a sigh of relief.

"At last! One day in the week where I don't have to be anywhere or see anybody! One day to myself to relax, daydream, contemplate the Mysteries of Life, or enjoy the simple pleasure of Doing Nothing at All!"

But Janet, being Janet, felt a little uneasy with a hole in the program, looked instead to see what clubs met that day, and decided on the Pep Club for lack of being anything better. Also being Janet, to join a club meant to be an officer in it, and by the usual natural selection process, since she was twice as smart as anybody else in the outfit and about a dozen times more energetic, she ended up running it.

The Pep Club mainly existed to give our teams some friendly faces in the stands at Away games to cheer for them, but it was also in charge of enthusiasm-building activities like pep rallies and making and putting up rah-rah-go-team-go posters in the halls just before games. The team mascot, Freddy Falcon, usually a Pep Club member in a bird suit who danced and cavorted with the cheerleaders on the sidelines at all the games, was handled out of Janet's office (or her locker, anyway), as well. Since I could fly, she had even talked me into being Freddy Falcon for the big Homecoming game and strutting my aerial stuff at halftime. I had gone along with it with considerable reluctance, and the rocks that stunt had shaken loose hadn't stopped falling yet.

"In fact," Janet went on, reaching into her notebook, "here's something that will tell you what's going on." She pulled out a flyer and let me read it.

SANTA CLAUS IS COMING TO TOWN — BY PARACHUTE!

That's right! Jolly old St. Nick will be dropping in at the New Romford Shopping Plaza parking lot at 11:00 am on Saturday, November 25, 1967!

CHILDREN OF ALL AGES ARE INVITED TO WELCOME SANTA CLAUS!

The 1967 Christmas Season officially begins here!

EXTRA ADDED ATTRACTION: Freddy Falcon will help Santa pass out a free gift to every child in attendance!

Musical entertainment will be provided by the New Romford High School Marching Band playing all your favorite Christmas songs!

Listen to Santa's arrival live on WNRO (1260 AM)!

Do all of your Christmas shopping at the New Romford Shopping Plaza where there's always acres of free parking!

SPONSORED BY THE NEW ROMFORD SHOPPING PLAZA MERCHANTS' ASSOCIATION.

Special promotional activities by arrangement with Buddy's Air Services, Mansfield, O.

NOTE: Freddy Falcon will not fly at this event.

"I'm glad they added the note," I said, giving the flyer back to Janet. "Don't want to get the little tykes' hopes up."

"Or start a riot," she added with a shudder, remembering what had happened at the football game where Freddy didn't fly, one week after the one where he did. "Susie Blair's doing pretty well as the new Freddy, by the way. You ought to come out just to see her."

"Sorry. That's Saturday morning and I have to collect."

Then I had an idea. I took a moment or two to remember the song and sort out the rhymes, then softly sang:

"You better not cry, you better not bilk,

"You better not cheat, 'cause I'm telling your ilk,

"Santa Claus is hit-ting the silk!"

Janet winced. "Uh, 'bilk'? 'Ilk'? You're kind of reaching, aren't you? Besides, I really don't think the last line absolutely has to rhyme with the first two."

Even so... somebody in a Santa Claus suit making a parachute jump from a plane to the shopping center parking lot? A fleeting thought crossed my mind as I turned my attention to the book on my desk — *That's just asking for trouble.*

Saturday, November 25

When I came downstairs for breakfast that morning, I glanced out the window.

"Oh no..." I said with a sinking heart, seeing the white yard outside. It had snowed during the night — not a lot, but enough to cover things and put the snowplows to work on the streets. Even though the sky had pretty much cleared up with only scattered clouds overhead, this did not look good since I would be outside and on my bike. It was going to be one wet and sloppy day.

After the glorious freedom from school on Thursday and Friday, with delivering the daily Columbus *Express* to my customers the only item on the schedule besides stuffing myself with turkey and pumpkin pie, it was back to the routine on Saturday morning.

I was learning to live in a state of acute cartoon-deprivation. I'd had the paper route for over two years now and my Saturday mornings were taken up with Collecting instead of what I really wanted to do, which was watch junk cartoons mixed with lots of toy and cereal commercials. The *Express* didn't send out a nice monthly bill so people could pay by mail, unfortunately. The paperboy (usually, though our New Romford *News-Banner* was delivered by a papergirl) had to go out every Saturday morning and hit up each customer personally for the weekly bill.

Since the *Express* was an out-of-town paper, even though it was a fine major metropolitan daily with excellent coverage of state and national news, most people in town just took the *News-Banner* on weekdays for the local news ("obituaries for people you know," as Dad said). As a result, I only had about thirty-odd customers for the daily *Express* scattered through my vast territory. On the other hand, the *News-Banner* didn't publish on Sundays and the *Express* did, so I had about 130 customers for the big fat Sunday edition with the funnies. A few customers paid monthly, and one old lady I never saw did it by the year (a few more like her and my life would have been a lot easier, and I could have watched more cartoons), but for the most part, I had to retrace the entire route and knock on one door after another all morning long. After lunch, I'd go downtown and pay my own weekly bill to Mr. Carlson at the *Express* office.

And so, with breakfast out of the way, I put my jacket on, grabbed my loose-leaf account book and my zippered red money bag with the Columbus *Express* logo printed on it, and went out to get my bike out of the garage. With the sun poking through scattered clouds, the temperature had gotten a bit above freezing, maybe as high as 35° or so. That just made the streets and sidewalks slushy without melting the snow on the ground very much.

Snow was pretty rare this early, making me wonder as a grade-school kid if that "Over the river and through the woods" tune with the "horse knows the way to carry the sleigh" line really was meant as a specifically Thanksgiving song. There was just enough snow to make riding a bike that much harder even though the streets were plowed.

Still, having the power to fly even made riding a bike a little easier since I could push it through snow. Besides lift, I had forward propulsion, controlled by muscle tension. When I tensed my muscles in the direction I wanted to go, I went there. It was sort of "reach out and I'll be there." I reached out and there I was. I could also brake by tensing backwards enough to counteract my forward momentum. Naturally, it had taken a while to get the hang of all this and be able to fine-tune the balance of lift and propulsion, not to mention just the right amount of muscle tension to do what I wanted to do. I remembered only too well the time that summer, early on in my flying practice, when I'd accidentally put myself into an uncontrollable corkscrew half a mile above the lights of New Romford, and they'd gotten a lot closer before I figured out how to break the spin. If nothing else, all this muscle tensing for the past few months had put me in the best shape of my life.

Most of New Romford was north of the Winamac River, but I didn't live there. Main Street crossed the river, then trisected a little further on into three roads that fanned out to the south. Cross streets appeared, spanning Martinsburg Road to the east, Newark Road down the middle, and Granville Road to the west. I lived on Parrott Street, between Newark Road and Granville Road, but my paper route covered the entire wedge of real estate from where Martinsburg Road split off from Newark Road clear out to Ames Street, the last residential street to the south before you hit open country. In other words, I didn't even live in my own territory.

I lived far enough south that it made sense to collect in reverse order from how I delivered the papers. I rode my bike across Newark Road and a couple of blocks south to Ames Street, then proceeded from one house to the next, knocking on doors and ringing doorbells, up Ames and down Adamson, up Parrott and down Delano, and so on, working my way north. Just street after street of little houses.

While I was tending to business, my mind concentrated entirely on the weekly ritual of extracting money from my customers, Janet was across town and dealing with her own problems. Not only was I not there for most of what happened, I wasn't even thinking about what might be going on. Janet and I compared notes later, however, and combined that with what else we heard, we managed to put the story together in some kind of order.

"Oh God!" Susie Blair exclaimed from the back seat of the car. "Look at that crowd! I'm scared already!"

Up front, Janet turned to look at the girl taking up most of the back seat in her bulky brown-feathered bird suit with a simulated letterman's sweater and a big **NR** on the front.

"Don't worry," she assured her. "You'll do fine."

Janet was her usual stylish self that morning, wearing a long white coat and knee-high boots. She looked older and more sophisticated than her actual sixteen, and could have passed for a young teacher. In fact, she had been mistaken for the Pep Club's Faculty Advisor more than once at various functions. Since the actual Faculty Advisor was pretty much letting Janet run the show anyway these days, it was understandable.

"Yeah, I want to get some good pictures of you passing out toys," said the boy driving, a Senior named Greg Buskirk who took photographs for the school newspaper and yearbook.

"I'm gonna look like such a dip..." groaned Susie. She had shoulder-length brown hair, wore glasses, and was even sort of pretty if you didn't mind her expression of looking like she'd had a stomachache all her life (and it was probably all *your* fault), but her head poking out of the open neck was startlingly small compared to the cumbersome Freddy suit. Susie sounded like she would have liked nothing better than to jump up and down on the goofily grinning bird head on the seat next to her.

"No, you're not," Janet insisted cheerily. "Come on, the kids love Freddy!"

Privately, Janet was hardly as cheerful as she sounded. She had been able to talk the reluctant Susie into being Freddy Falcon after the precipitous departure of the previous incumbent, but *keeping* Susie talked into it was beginning to strain her powers of persuasion.

The New Romford Shopping Plaza was on the far northeast side of town, practically out in the country. It was a line of stores with a Big Bear supermarket as the anchor at the east end, fronted by a big parking lot. ("Big Bear" was just the name of the supermarket chain. Despite the name and the picture of a bear on the big sign, there weren't any bears inside, which always kind of disappointed me.) Now that Thanksgiving was behind us, the stores were already festooned with Christmas decorations, and large lighted ornaments in the shape of candy canes, snowmen, and tin soldiers were hung at the tops of the light poles.

After the previous night's snow, the plows had been at work to clear the parking lot, so there were piles of snow out by the road and at the side of the Big Bear store. Usually there was a lot more lot than there were cars to fill it, so there was room for special events, like carnivals or antique car shows or whatever.

For this particular event, the advance publicity had done its job since the lot was almost filled with cars and a fair-sized mob of children and their parents was already on hand, surrounding the roped-off area marked as the drop zone. A couple of policemen circulated through the crowd, but with little to do since nobody was being particularly unruly. Meanwhile, a concession booth was doing a brisk business selling candy and goodies to the kids and cups of coffee to their shivering parents. The high school band was there, too, setting up by a school bus.

Greg parked the car in a far corner of the lot where a few open spaces were left. Then Janet had to help Susie maneuver out of the back seat. Bulky as the costume was, she had trouble getting out of a confined space with anything like dignity, especially since Greg's car was a two-door and she had to climb over the folded-down front seatback.

"Take it easy," Janet told her, pulling her by one arm through the open door. "We don't want to bend the tail."

"You try doing anything in this get-up," Susie griped.

"Just be glad we don't drive you around in the back of a pickup truck," Janet replied, a little annoyed.

"Well, it'd be easier to get in and out of," Susie snapped.

Greg went off to take some general background pictures while Janet led Susie, carrying the Freddy head under her arm, across the lot towards the crowd, hoping to find someone there who could tell them what to do next. As it happened, that someone found them.

A middle-aged woman with a clipboard in hand came up. That was Mrs. Stigler, who mostly worked as a secretary for the shopping center's manager but also had the thankless job of being Director of Special Promotional Events.

"Oh good, you're here," she said, checking something off on her list of things to do. "Put the head on, dear. We don't want to traumatize the children by seeing Freddy with his head off."

"Aww, it messes up my hair..." Susie muttered.

"What do you want us to do, exactly?" Janet asked quickly, before Mrs. Stigler could think to ask why, if that was a problem, Susie wanted to be Freddy in the first place and Susie would start to wonder about that, too.

"Well, we can't pass out the toys until Santa gets here," Mrs. Stigler said, "but maybe Freddy can mingle with the crowd and say hi to the kids.

You know, keep them busy and not getting too restless while they're waiting."

"Uh... before we do that," Susie spoke up, "is there, well, a ladies' room or something like that around here?"

"Why didn't you think of that before we left?" Janet demanded, exasperated. "You know what a pain it is to get the costume off for that."

"I didn't have to go before we left," Susie shot back, "but I sure do now."

"Come with me," Mrs. Stigler said resignedly, sounding like she had way too much to do already and this was just one more thing. "There's a bathroom in my office but I'll have to unlock it for you." She started across the lot towards the Big Bear store, with Susie clumping in her big yellow bird feet behind her.

That left Janet by herself. Feeling a bit chilly in the cold air, she decided to use her unexpected free time to get a warming cup from the concession booth.

Just as the counterman was handing her the hot chocolate she'd asked for, an old man wearing a fedora and a long coat stepped up to the booth.

"A cup of coffee, please," he called, then turned to her. "Good morning, Miss Larsen," he said pleasantly, touching the brim of his hat. "We meet again."

It was Clyde Harbaugh, the reporter from the *News-Banner* who covered the local beat for events like this (*I'd know that bow-tie anywhere*, Janet thought). After the Freddy Falcon stunt at the Homecoming game, Mr. Harbaugh had tried to talk to her a couple of times for more details about how the trick was done. She and her parents had put him off so far, but old newshound that he was, he apparently sensed that there was a story buried somewhere and it took more than weak excuses and muddled explanations to satisfy him.

"Er...hello, Mr. Harbaugh," Janet replied with the decent amount of politeness.

"I'm sorry to hear Freddy Falcon won't be flying today," he said with a slightly bogus-sounding sigh for effect. "I would have liked to see that again."

"So would everybody else, but I'm afraid Homecoming was all we could manage," Janet said quickly. "Well, I'd love to stay and chat, but I have to take this to somebody before it gets cold." She grabbed her hot chocolate and lost herself in the crowd before Harbaugh could start asking inconvenient questions.

Janet then went by the WNRO table. Santa Claus coming to town by parachute was a big deal, so the local radio station had sent out the mobile unit to cover it live. The WNRO van was backed up against the edge of the marked-off circle where Santa was supposed to land. The rear doors were open and a technician was inside adjusting things on control panels, while a loudspeaker on top of the truck was relaying the studio broadcast, currently playing "Jingle Bell Rock."

A banner on the side of the truck read: "WNRO — Where the Action is!!!" If "the Action" was someplace where teenagers were hopping and bopping, WNRO usually wasn't anywhere in the neighborhood. The station's bill of fare was mostly stuff you'd have to be over 50 to want to listen to: farm reports, news, syndicated shows like Paul Harvey, tons of commercials, and a very occasional song, usually by the likes of Perry Como. The station's main attempt to grab the under-50 audience was a two-hour program on Saturday morning called "Teen Time," hosted by a couple of kids I knew, but I was out collecting then and could never listen to it. Since this was a live news event, it looked as though the kids were taking the day off.

Between the van and the drop zone, a folding table and three chairs had been set up. In the middle, facing a microphone, sat the announcer, a rather overweight middle-aged man with a grey-flecked beard. That was Rick Fairfield (but was it his real name or just his *nom de broadcast*?), WNRO's morning show host and news director. How much news he had to direct was a good question. People who got the *Clarion-Journal* (the Columbus morning paper — like Marvo the Clown said on TV, you could read the CJ while drinking OJ in your PJs) claimed they could follow right along as RF announced the AM news. On one side of him was an empty chair for anybody he managed to snag for an on-air interview, while on the other side sat a pretty lady in charge of passing out goodies.

As Janet passed the table, the pretty lady gave her a free 45-rpm record. It was obviously years old and Janet had never heard of the song or the performer, and it was clearly marked "**PROMOTIONAL USE ONLY / NOT FOR SALE**." Was the station both trying to clean out its closet and score points by giving out free stuff it had gotten for free itself?

If things were going according to schedule, two men should have been walking towards a small airplane out at Kane County Airport about now. One would have been Buddy, the pilot and proprietor of Buddy's Air

Services. The other would be Mel, his partner, a large man wearing a parachute pack strapped on over a Santa Claus suit.

They were professionals. They had already done this stunt several times in different towns around Ohio in the last week. Perhaps Mel was a little too young to be very believable as Santa Claus even with the white beard, but the kiddies never seemed to notice and it was a better gig than unloading truck tires or running a punch press. The main thing was that the local merchants who hired them loved the publicity the promotional stunt brought with it. Seeing Santa Claus arrive by parachute made the children excited and happy. Seeing the children excited and happy gave the parents a warm Christmas feeling. Parents with a warm Christmas feeling tended to buy more presents from the nice stores that sponsored the event. That gave the merchants a warm Christmas feeling of their own, which could be expressed in just a few words: "Pay to the Order of Buddy's Air Services."

By this time, Buddy and Mel would be climbing into the plane. Not needing much padding to play Santa and wearing a parachute, Mel would have had more trouble than Buddy getting through the small door and settling into the cramped little seat. Then Buddy would be preparing for take-off.

With jump-time only minutes away, the school band was finally up and ready. The director motioned to Mrs. Stigler. She checked her watch and nodded. The director raised his arms and the band launched into a rousing rendition of "Jingle Bells." The spectators realized something was about to happen and pressed closer to the roped-off area.

Meanwhile, Freddy Falcon was working the crowd, shaking hands with the children, dancing a little, and generally clowning around. Janet followed a little behind, mostly to make sure older kids didn't give Susie a hard time by trying to trip her or pull the head off. The only thing was, Susie wasn't very good at being Freddy. She was nervous, reluctant to really get up close and personal with the kids, just going through the motions and obviously wishing she was somewhere else. Janet found herself missing Patti Wilcox, the former Freddy. For all her disagreeable qualities, stuff Patti into the suit and she was positively inspired. Susie was just disagreeable in or out of the suit.

Maybe I should start thinking about trying to get Patti back, Janet thought reluctantly. *I'd hate to have to work with her again, but she's just too darned good at it...*

Janet was near the WNRO table when the show got under way. As "Jingle Bells" faded out, Rick Fairfield spoke into the microphone and his voice went out over the van's loudspeakers.

"Hi, kids! I'm glad to see all of you here to help welcome Santa Claus to the New Romford Shopping Plaza, with twelve different stores to help your mommies and daddies find all sorts of wonderful Christmas presents! In fact, I have Santa on the radio right now, waiting to talk to you! Come in, Santa Claus!"

Another voice crackled over the loudspeakers, this one rather affectedly hearty but somewhat muffled by a background droning.

"Jumpin' jingle bells! Merry Christmas, boys and girls! This is Santa Claus! I left my reindeer at home today, but I'm going to come visit you the modern way! Ho ho ho!"

From down on the ground, the black spot of an approaching plane could be seen in the distance. The crowd murmured and people pointed.

"Well, I'm about to jump now!" Santa announced. "I'm opening the door—"

The plane came closer, but it was still so high up that it was just a speck in the sky.

"Here I come, ready or not!" Santa added, his voice almost lost in now louder background noise, probably the rushing wind from the open door. "Ho, ho—"

BLOOMPH!

A sudden burst of radio crackles and static followed, mixed with a couple of unprintable obscenities.

As things quieted down a bit, a different voice that had to be Buddy the pilot cut through the noise.

"Oh my God! Mel caught his ripcord on something! His chute opened before he could jump and the wind pulled him right out! Took the door with him... His chute's wrapped around the right wheel and he's being dragged along! I can hardly hold the plane steady with that weight hanging off the side!"

The crowd gasped. Some children started crying. Janet stayed where she was, listening in horrified fascination. Overhead, the plane went on its way, too high to see anything of what was happening from the ground.

There was a pause as Buddy apparently listened to something they were telling him from the airport. That side of the conversation wasn't being picked up on WNRO's broadcast.

"Look, dammit!" Buddy suddenly exploded. "How can I land with Mel hanging back there? I can't take my hands off the yoke to pull him in! I can barely keep it steady as it is! And if I go any slower, I'll stall!"

Another pause. Then — "Why can't he jettison his main and use his reserve? Because I think he's unconscious, that's why!"

Rick Fairfield's newscasting career may have been mainly reading articles in the paper out loud, but he must have had some journalistic

106

instincts and for once WNRO really was where the action was. He grabbed the mike.

"This is Rick Fairfield, broadcasting live from the New Romford Shopping Plaza, where a dramatic story is now in progress! The joy in the eyes of countless Kane County children has just turned to tears as tragedy threatens to strike a happy holiday occasion!" And on and on like that.

Meanwhile, Janet's first thought was, *Kyle!* She whirled, pushed through the crowd, and broke into a run across the parking lot to the Big Bear store. Near the doors, mounted on the outside wall, were a couple of pay phones. Janet found a dime in her purse along with her address book and dialed a number.

A woman answered. "Millses."

Janet knew me well enough to know that Mills was my stepfather's name. "Is Kyle there?" she blurted.

"No, he's out collecting for his paper route. Can I take a message?"

"That's okay, Mrs. Mills. I'll find him some other way." *I hope*, Janet added to herself. Then she called her own number. When her father answered, she exclaimed, "Dad! Has Kyle Rhodebeck been by to collect for the paper?"

"That's the *Express* kid, isn't it? Nope, not yet."

"You've got to find him! It's a life and death situation here!"

"All right, but how? I barely know the kid."

Janet had that already worked out. "His mother told me he's out collecting for his paper route, and I know his route covers everything between Martinsburg Road and Newark Road. Just drive up and down the cross streets until you see him!"

"And what do I tell him if I do?"

Janet quickly described what was going on. "Tune the car radio to WNRO," she added. "They're covering it live and you'll get the details. Would you please hurry?!"

"On my way," Mr. Larsen said.

When Janet pushed her way back through the rapidly thinning crowd — a lot of parents evidently didn't want their kids around and listening if the story ended anything like the way it looked only too likely to end — she passed the WNRO table where Clyde Harbaugh was sitting next to Rick Fairfield and being interviewed.

After rehashing what had happened for those listeners who had just joined us, Fairfield then had the problem of filling air time. If Buddy was just going to fly in a wide circle over New Romford until Mel came to and got loose on his own or somebody thought of something else, not a whole lot would be going on for a while, and Fairfield had a live microphone in front of him. Interviewing whoever was handy for some hopefully at least somewhat relevant insights was about all he could do.

"Well, Mr. Harbaugh," he was saying, "you've been a reporter in this area all your life. Can you think of any news events quite as dramatic as this one during your long career?"

Harbaugh thought, taking his hat off and scratching his thinning white hair. "About the only thing I can think of that quite compares with this was a bank robbery back in the '30s, where the crooks took one of the tellers hostage and drove off with him..."

Janet went on and found Susie standing by the school bus and at loose ends. With most people clearing out and certainly not in the mood for funny falconry anymore, that left her with nothing to do.

As Janet came up, a very tiny little girl passing by with her mother suddenly scurried over to Susie and tugged on the costume. As Susie awkwardly bent down — she could only see straight ahead through a screen at the back of the perpetually open beak — the tot looked up at her earnestly with tears streaming down her cheeks.

"Pwease, Fweddy, can't you fwy and save Santa?"

"But I *can't* fly!" Susie burst out in frustration, her voice ringing hollowly inside the falcon head.

"You fwoo at da big game!" the little girl insisted.

"That was a *different* Freddy!" Susie shot back. Suddenly, she tore the Freddy head off and went stomping away. "I've had it! I quit!" She glanced back at Janet with venom in her eyes. "I never should've let you talk me into this in the first place!"

Patti may get her old job back yet, Janet thought a little helplessly. *But if I let Susie cool down, maybe I can talk to her later...*

Seeing Freddy come apart, not to mention getting the full blast of Susie's anger, the little girl burst out howling. Her mother was coming over to them, looking furious, but Janet bent down and held the girl for a moment.

"Don't worry!" she told her. "The other Freddy is on the way! I called him just now. He'll save Santa!" *I hope.*

"Weally?" the little girl sniffled as she choked back a sob, calming down somewhat.

"Yes, weally! I mean, *really!*"

That seemed to comfort the little girl. Then her mother took charge of her, not looking at all happy but probably not exactly sure who deserved yelling at or for what, and led her away. The girl looked back at Janet and waved, smiling through her tears, then stuck her tongue out at the Freddy who couldn't fly.

Janet looked up at the bright blue sky. *Please, Dad! Find Kyle! Fast!*

I was just coming out of the Daughertys' attached garage on Pine Street, a little east of Elmwood School, my old elementary alma mater, and a little west of Martinsburg Road. These wonderful people had a nail in their garage wall by the door to the house, and hung their *Express* payment envelope there. All I had to do was go into the garage side door, which was never locked, take the money that was in the envelope, mark their card and my book, and I was off. No knocking, no bother about having to catch them at home...

As I closed the door behind me, a red Mustang pulled into the driveway. The driver stopped, opened the door, and half got out, the engine still running. "Kyle! We've got trouble!"

I recognized Janet's father at once, a trim 40ish man who worked in one of the local factories. What kind of trouble he could have that he would go looking for me, I couldn't imagine. My fleeting guess was that something had gone wrong with the new Freddy Falcon at that Shopping Plaza doings, but I had no idea why Janet would roust me for that. I had made it clear there was no way in heck I would ever put that dumb bird suit on again.

"Get in," Mr. Larsen added, pointing to the passenger side of the car. "I'll explain on the way."

I was completely baffled, but Mr. Larsen wouldn't be here like this if it wasn't important. I left my bike where it stood on its kickstand on the sidewalk by the Daughertys' garage door. They would know whose it was even if they were puzzled why I had left it there for a while.

I got into the Mustang and Mr. Larsen was backing out of the driveway even before I could close the door completely. He had the radio on and I heard a crackling voice.

"...What the hell am I supposed to do? Fly around until I run out of gas? Great — get us both killed instead of just Mel!"

I was astonished, though at first mostly because I had never heard the h-e-double-hockey-sticks word spoken on the radio before.

"What the heck?" I asked Mr. Larsen.

He gave me a quick summary of the situation. Somewhere up there was a small airplane dragging an unconscious Santa Claus through the air behind it, with the canopy of his parachute wrapped around one of the wheels.

"Wow..." I murmured as the image sank in. "So you thought of me?"

"Well, Janet did. Look, kid, I don't know how you can do what I've seen you do, and I can't make sense of what Janet's told me about it. All I know is that Janet thinks somebody's going to die unless you do something."

Dwight R. Decker

I swallowed hard. I had gotten the Call. It reminded me of what Dad had said about working for his father as an ambulance driver before the War. Grandpa was an undertaker and funeral homes handled ambulance services in small towns in Ohio. More than a few times, the phone had rung at something like 3:00 am, waking Dad up and sending him out on an emergency. It wasn't being a Hero, it was having a Responsibility. He had an ambulance, so he had to do the job. Me, I had a flying unit in my chest. I had it, no one else did, so the call came for me.

"Where do you want me to let you out?" Mr. Larsen asked.

I thought. Since I wanted to keep the flying power something like a secret, daylight take-offs in the middle of the old neighborhood were a bit of a problem. He could have driven me out into the country so I could take off where nobody was around to see me, but we didn't have much time.

Then I had an idea. "Take me back to your house!"

Mr. Larsen looked a little puzzled, but that's where he took me. I had my reasons. Meanwhile, I told him to keep an eye on my account book and my money bag until I got back.

The Larsens lived in a little gray house on Cliff Street, just east of Martinsburg Road and a little north of Pine. The name wasn't a poetic fancy on the part of some old-time developer since Janet's house really was on a cliff. Umpteen thousand years ago, it would have been beachfront property, as it was perched at the edge of a dry lakebed about a mile across. Now, cornfields stretched where the waves of Lake Winamac once rippled. (Not that the lake was entirely extinct. During the Great Flood of 1959, the Winamac River overflowed its banks and flooded the bottomland, and for a time Lake Winamac lived again.)

Mr. Larsen turned into his driveway, and I was out of the car before he could stop. I vaulted the chain-link fence in front of the house and sprinted across the side yard. Ahead of me was the back fence and just empty space. There was nothing else beyond except a steep drop of about twenty feet and a mile or so of snow-covered bottomland until you got to the river and the hills rising on the other side. Then I leaped over the back fence and plunged into the void. Lord only knew what Mr. Larsen was thinking if he was watching me, and I wasn't sure exactly how much Janet had told her parents, though she had assured me that she had them sworn to utmost secrecy about what they did know.

The power surged and the flying unit went into action. I arched over the bushes and small trees at the bottom of the cliff, then I thrust my arms forward and leveled out just a few feet above the ground, and shot off across the bottomland towards the river a mile away. Cold wind tore at my hair and I struggled to keep my glasses on.

110

I was zipping over the stumps of cornstalks poking up through the snow, punching through the air resistance like a human torpedo. By keeping low to the cornfield, I was hoping that anyone who happened to be looking this way wouldn't know what they were seeing even if they spotted something moving out in the bottomland.

Then I shot across the river not far from the sewage plant and went into the hills. The slopes were heavily wooded with just a few scattered houses. Even with the trees bare at this time of year, they gave me cover. My idea was to avoid being noticed when I went for altitude. A human being alone in the empty sky could be seen for miles, and I was especially at risk during take-offs and landings when I was close to the ground.

I went into an upward spiral around the back of a hill, then threw myself into a steep climb, piling on the speed to get up to the higher elevations as fast as I could and keep short the time I was most visible. I could probably still be seen as a black speck when I was way up there, but if anybody saw me then, they'd think I was a bird or something. The Mystery Bird sightings had died down in the last few months, once I'd gotten a little more discreet about daylight flying, and I could only hope this wouldn't start them up again.

As I rose, the world beneath me flattened out, turning from the busy, cluttered, crowded surroundings I usually lived in to a thin layer far below. Most of what we do is in the first twenty feet or so, and there's an awful lot of emptiness overhead. This was the first time I had flown in daylight with snow on the ground, and the sheer *brightness* was almost stunning as I soared through the achingly blue sky high above snowfields dazzling in the sunlight.

Meanwhile, the sky around me turned 3-D. Since we're on the ground looking up at the bottoms of clouds, we don't notice something that's really striking when you get up on a level with them as I now was with just a few small clouds around me. Clouds are in layers, like cotton wads drifting across a giant glass sheet. I guess it has to do with different temperatures at different heights, so the same kind of clouds would form at the same altitude.

I felt exhilarated for a moment. It wasn't often I had a chance to fly during the day, and even chilly as it was, the bright sunlight was invigorating. Even so, I wasn't Mighty Mouse, and I resisted my urge to shout, "Here I come to save the day!" I was just a fifteen-year-old kid with a job to do, and didn't have time to worry about dramatic flourishes.

At about a thousand feet, I slowed my climb and tried to get my bearings, fighting somewhat to hold steady against a cold, stiff wind out of the west. The crosshatch of streets against the white background looked more like a map than ever. To the north and east was the curving ribbon of the

Winamac River, and on the other side the main part of New Romford. I had started on the south side of town and a little east. The Shopping Plaza was well to the northeast, and in fact, with all of New Romford spread out below me, I could pick it out easily enough (the "acres of free parking" were kind of obvious even from here). The next problem was finding the plane.

I had gotten the impression from what Mr. Larsen had told me and what little I'd heard on the radio that the pilot was flying a wide circle around New Romford while waiting for help, though nobody had figured out yet just what that was going to be. That meant I should be able to spot the plane. There wasn't much else up here, and if I could be seen for miles around, a plane was quite a bit bigger than I was.

Then, way off to the northwest, I saw a moving speck. Had to be it. I went into horizontal flight and headed off in that direction.

When I flew straight out like this, I sometimes wondered if this was what surfing was like. Two or three years back, surf music had been big on the radio, and being landlocked in Central Oh., my pals and I had liked the driving guitar music but were kind of unclear on exactly what the words meant. Sometimes I had listened to a surfing song like Jan & Dean's "Ride the Wild Surf" and imagined myself flying. Now I was flying and imagining "Ride the Wild Surf" playing in the background. But in real life the only sound was the swoosh of the wind past my ears.

Every other time I'd flown in daylight, I'd made sure to avoid going anywhere near small planes so I wouldn't be seen. This was the first time I'd ever had to approach one. I didn't want the pilot to see me, so I went up a little in order to overtake the plane from above and behind. My usual cruising speed was about 60 mph, not because I couldn't go any faster but because air resistance got to be too much of a bother to comfortably fight through. At a guess, this guy was doing well over a hundred, actually kind of slow for a plane but faster than I liked to go, and I had to hit the gas to catch up.

As I came closer to the plane, I saw what we had here. It was a small high-winged Cessna, barely big enough for two people upfront and maybe a third in the back. Somebody in a red suit was hanging off the side and to the rear, dragged along by cords trailing from the parachute canopy wrapped around the right front wheel. The plane was a little tipped from the weight of the dangling man, and it looked as though the pilot was having all he could do to fly straight and steady. To add to his problems, the right-hand door was gone.

The closer I got, the more I began to worry. Just how was I supposed to do this? Getting a man untangled from a parachute and then safely down to the ground wasn't going to be quite as easy as, say, getting a cat out of a tree.

I dropped down just behind the plane, and straining my arms out to the utmost, I caught up with the trailing Santa. He was hanging limp in his harness as he was being yanked along headfirst and face down by the lines from the parachute pack, and looked unconscious. I wouldn't be able to keep my speed up and work on getting him loose at the same time, so I grabbed on to the straps of his parachute pack and let the plane pull me along. With the chill wind tearing at me, I slipped my left arm underneath one of the straps to hang on, letting me have my right arm free.

"Something's going on," Buddy's voice choked over the radio. "I can't see what it is, but all of a sudden there's a hell of a lot more drag. I can hardly hold the plane steady. Christ, I hope his reserve didn't open, too!"

First, I checked to make sure that Santa was still alive. It looked like he'd been whacked but good going out the door. There was a nasty cut on his forehead and his nose was probably broken, with blood staining his beard almost as red as his suit. At least he seemed to be still with us, if knocked out. I was a little amazed that his beard and hat had stayed on through all that, but since he was making a parachute jump with them on, he'd probably made an extra effort to pin them firmly in place. Santa landing in front of all those kids with pieces missing would have spoiled the effect, after all.

Then I looked to see what I had to do to get Mr. Claus loose. One thing was clear. I really should have brought a knife. I had one for cutting the twine on bundles of newspapers on Sundays, but I had left it at home. The canopy was thoroughly wrapped around the wheel, and untangling it looked like an all-day job. I had no idea how parachutes worked, so if there was a way to disconnect the pack from the cords, I didn't know what it was. As far as I could see, the only quick and easy solution to the problem was to unbuckle the pack and pull the guy out of it entirely.

He seemed to be sitting on some kind of sling-like strap that ran under his heinie, with a strap under each leg at the crotch to keep him from falling out. The leg straps ran up his body and over his shoulders, buckled together by a couple of short horizontal straps across his chest. I started undoing the clasps—

And undid one clasp too many. Before I could grab him, Santa dropped out of the harness. To my punched-in-the-stomach horror, he fell away from me and plunged straight down, belly-first, arms and legs limply

raised by the air resistance, shrinking fast against the snow-draped coun-
tryside not so very far below.

Suddenly freed of Santa's drag, the plane lurched forward. I lost my
grip on the harness and was left behind.

The effect would have been obvious at once to Buddy inside the cock-
pit, when he suddenly found himself flying a steady plane. The reason why
and what must have happened would have also been obvious.

At the Shopping Plaza, Buddy's voice crackled over the WNRO
van's speakers. "Oh no! I just lost him!" Pause. "Maybe he came to and
got loose on his own and used his reserve. I'll check." Another pause.
"Christ... His pack's still here! I don't know how but he must have fallen
out of the harness!"

Everyone standing around and listening gasped. Then there were
sobs. A few of the remaining parents turned and pulled their kids away.

I threw myself into a power dive, shooting down faster than I would
have dropped in simple free fall, aiming for the spread-eagled, red-suited
figure slowly spinning below me. I had to catch up with Santa and the
ground was coming up fast.

Forget what you've seen in the comic books where Lois falls 95 stories off a building and Superman catches her just before she hits the sidewalk. At that point, a sudden stop in Supes' arms might as well be hitting
the concrete (really putting the "terminal" in "terminal velocity"). Since I
wasn't Superman, the effect on me would be kind of drastic, too. Instead,
I had to match speeds with Santa, grab on to something solid — his belt
looked substantial enough — and brake gradually. But not too gradually.
I did want to bring him to a complete stop somewhere on this side of
ground level.

It wasn't easy. I was a husky lad and had carried Janet on my back
without breathing hard, but this guy hadn't had to stuff any pillows under
his coat to look the part, and all his weight was pulling on my arms and
shoulders instead of being spread out more evenly. Even if the flying unit
had enough power to lift a battleship, it wouldn't do me any good if my
arms were pulled out of their sockets.

Slowing this human lardbucket down was taking a heck of a lot longer
than I liked. As my panic started to mount, I vaguely noticed that we were
somewhere out in the country. Snow-covered fields and black woodlots
were spread out beneath us, getting closer all the time.

Clutching his belt, I clenched my teeth and strained to brake both of
us. The pull on my fingers, hands, and arms was tremendous, since I had
to compensate for our combined weight. The ground was getting awfully

close and I began to think a horrible thought. I might have to let Santa go and pull out of the fall myself, or we'd both slam into the dirt. But I couldn't just let the guy die. I'd have to explain it to Janet afterwards and live with it for the rest of my life. I strained against the weight all the harder, aching fingers and arms and all. Finally, we slowed enough and just in time to touch down lightly in a snowy field, and fortunately nobody was around to see us.

Now that I had him, what do I do with him? Drop him off somewhere and find a phone to call somebody to come out and pick him up? But that could take a while and he was obviously hurt. Flying him straight into town to the hospital risked being seen and too many questions.

Then I had an idea. The Shopping Plaza was far enough out of town that there wasn't much of anything around it, especially behind it to the north. I could go around the far northern outskirts of New Romford and come in behind the shopping center without too much danger of anyone spotting me. If nothing else, carrying Santa Claus would give me such a strange silhouette that anyone seeing me from any distance wouldn't know what I was.

The only thing was, my arms were aching. I wouldn't be able to carry Santa very far if I did it the same way I got him down. And since he was unconscious, he was pure dead weight, unable to cooperate by hanging on. The only way to do this seemed to be to spread his weight out over my back instead of trying to support him with just my arms. I got under him in a sort of fireman's carry and managed a clumsy, wobbly take-off.

Once we were up, it wasn't so bad. With his weight evenly distributed on top of me instead of pulling my arms loose, I could support him comfortably and even get up some speed. It was easier on my arms to hold him on than to hold him up. We were somewhere west of New Romford, so I swung in a wide arc to the northeast to avoid the built-up areas where I might be seen.

A few minutes later, I was flying in low over the trees in a woodlot just behind the shopping center. To my relief, I spotted a high mound of snow piled up by the plows at the east side of the Big Bear store on the end. I slowed up, approached the snowpile, and paused at the top of it just long enough to gently set Santa down on his back. He was still unconscious, but starting to stir a little. Then I slid down the snow and came to my feet on the parking lot. Some distance away, towards the Coshocton Road end of the lot, I saw a school bus, the WNRO van, a couple of police cars, and a few people milling around. That seemed like the likeliest place to find Janet, so I trotted in that direction.

When I arrived, I found the school band packing up, and whatever crowd of parents and kids had gathered here was fairly well gone. Everybody seemed stunned and silent.

I found Janet by the band bus, talking to Susie Blair, who was wearing the body of the Freddy costume but with the head off. (*Spoil the illusion for the kiddies, why don't you*, I thought.)

Janet saw me coming and turned towards me with a bleak and devastated look. "Oh, Kyle... I guess Dad didn't find you in time..." I had never seen her at such a loss.

"*Au contraire, ma chère*," I said, getting some use out of what I was learning in French III to keep from spilling the beans to Susie. I jerked my thumb back to point to the side of the Big Bear store. "I don't know if he's the one you're looking for, but there's some guy in a Santa suit lying on top of that pile of snow over there."

It was like a light suddenly snapped on inside of Janet. "Thank God!" she blurted and gave me a quick hug, then ran off to tell somebody in charge.

That left Susie standing by herself in the bird costume and looking confused. "Nice suit," I commented.

She gave me a sour look. "You try wearing this thing!"

Actually, I had worn it, but that was supposed to be a secret and I let it drop.

Meanwhile, I saw Janet leading a group of people to the snowpile where I'd left Santa, so events would take their course from here without me. I headed towards the back of the shopping center to find a nice, secluded place to take off.

Pine Street stopped at Martinsburg Road, and on the other side was a church with nothing but cornfields beyond it to the east. I came in behind the church, landed, and walked the rest of the way to the Daughertys' house to pick up my bike. It was still where I had left it, and I rode over to Janet's house to pick up my money bag and account book so I could get back to collecting.

"Just heard on the radio they found the guy safe and sound," Mr. Larsen said when he answered the door. "So I guess you took care of things."

"Pretty much," I said as he gave me my stuff. "Uhm... while I'm here and just so I don't have to come back..."

Mr. Larsen sighed and reached into his pocket. "I'll get the card."

For me, that was the end of it. I had a paper route to take care of. I went on my way happy to have done something a little more important than getting a cat down from a tree, even though only Janet and her father knew what I'd done. For other people, the controversy simmered for days.

Clyde Harbaugh wrote a nice column for the *News-Banner* about Christmas miracles, saying it would have been a pretty rotten Christmas for all the kids in New Romford and Kane County if Santa Claus had gotten splattered across the Ohio landscape practically right in front of them (though he didn't really use the word "splattered"). Nobody quite understood why Mel was still alive and recovering nicely at Mercy Hospital from nothing more serious than a broken nose and a mild concussion, but how could you argue with a miracle?

The members of the New Romford Shopping Plaza Merchants' Association weren't quite so holly-jolly about it, however. They had contracted with Buddy's Air Services for one (1) parachute jump by an individual dressed like Santa Claus, and as far as they were concerned, Buddy hadn't delivered.

In fact, one rumor around town had it that the whole thing had been staged, since nobody had actually seen Mel fall. Maybe he had never intended to jump and was never even in the plane. Like it was a cover story for him showing up too drunk to jump or something. After all, if Mel really had been hung up like Buddy said, how could he fall hundreds of feet onto a pile of snow and live?

So there things stayed. If it was all a fraud, it was a strange one that had left Buddy a lot worse off, with no pay for the job and a damaged airplane. People scratched their heads over the mystery, but finally gave up, saying "There must be more to it than They ever said," and went on to other things.

Thank goodness for the ever-mysterious They, the all-purpose pronoun for the unspecified Powers That Be who ran things. I always imagined They as a wise council of supermen who sat in solemn conclave and made decisions no one outside their sacred precincts could fathom. For the sake of my secret, it was handy to have Them around to blame minor little mysteries on.

But Mel was alive. That was the main thing. I'm not sure if I saved Christmas, exactly, but at least the little squirts of New Romford had been spared witnessing the death of Santa Claus. That ought to count for something.

Cover of the original fanzine-style Christmas mailing as illustrated by the Author himself and featuring his dog and bird characters Woofer and Tweeter. Perhaps some Authors should stick to writing and leave the drawing to trained professionals.

Christmas Carol Critique

Introduction

"Christmas Carol Critique" was sent out with the cards some years back as well as printed in my fanzine of the time. As explained in the lead-in, it was the result of a few too many years listening to the same radio station's playlist and starting to think about the lyrics.

Some people thought my musical musings were amusing, but at least one reaction heaved with scorn for my spending so much time and thought on something so silly and trivial. Did my eggnog go bad on me and spoil my holiday mood? The songs are just beloved Christmas favorites — you're not *supposed* to think about them too much! Where that rule is carved in stone was not stated.

Well, *I* had a good time doing it. This little Christmas-themed volume seemed like a good place to present the piece to a larger audience with some editorial fine-tuning and even a bit of new content. In particular, the write-ups for "Last Christmas and "Little Drummer Boy" are new for this edition.

These, of course, are my opinions, and as the saying goes, your mileage may differ, and probably will.

Christmas Carol Critique

Working at home, I listen to a lot of radio. Usually I have it tuned to a Chicago station that plays Adult Contemporary mixed with '80s oldies. Most of the year, anyway. In November, the station converts to "holiday mode" and plays non-stop Christmas music.

This makes quite a few years now that I've been listening to tons of Christmas songs, mostly the same ones over and over. According to the station's website, the playlist is just over 200 titles, which may sound like a lot but not when they're played repeatedly day after day for weeks on end. Most of the songs are pop versions by contemporary artists, many taken from the *A Very Special Christmas* series of CDs done circa 1992 to benefit the Special Olympics and still available.

After a while the lyrics start to sink in. It's dawned on me that some of these sentimental favorites make little or no sense. Somebody was trying too hard to crowbar in a rhyme, or a song with a winter theme but nothing in particular to do with Christmas was adopted somewhere along the line as fitting the season. So it's no surprise that I've formed a few opinions about some of these songs, which I will proceed to express. I should point out that there are multiple variants of even the old standards, with slight changes in the lyrics from one recorded version to another.

Before starting, what exactly *is* a Christmas carol, anyway? I remember being fairly confused on that point as a lad, if only because my mother's kid sister was named Carol. Why were groups of people going from house to house singing about Aunt Carol? I mean she lived in Illinois and we lived in Ohio. How did they even know her?

To solve the mystery, we need only consult the learned Mr. Webster. "Carol" in this sense comes from Latin and ultimately Greek, and is related to the word "chorus." Definitions include "a song of joy and mirth" and "a popular song or ballad of religious joy." That seems to fit, although it might be debatable whether many of the more popular or secular songs that follow are strictly speaking "carols" at all. For that matter, I've always been puzzled as to why Mr. Dickens entitled his not very musical ghost story *A Christmas Carol*.

Now let's get to it…

Grandma Got Run Over by a Reindeer
Written by Randy Brooks
1979
Elmo & Patsy

It was possibly funny the first time, but after years of repetition, it's grown a little thin. The man's grandmother has been killed in a freak accident and he's yukking it up. An animated adaptation was made in which Grandma survives, and I've been told the same is true of a live-action video version, but in the song itself it's pretty definite that she is no longer oxygen-dependent.

Maybe it's good ol' boy humor, pretending to be unperturbed by something that rightly should shake you up, and making crass jokes about it to show it doesn't bother you because you're so tuff and cool. Then again, I remember that kind of humor being prevalent among my circle of cronies when I was about fourteen, so maybe fourteen-year-old boys (in spirit if not necessarily in body) are in fact the primary audience for this song.

I've seen figures on how much "Elmo" (a retired veterinarian) takes in per year in royalties on this one-hit wonder as it's played each year, and it's probably a lot more than he ever made alleviating the suffering of quadrupeds. (Though the misery the song causes us bipeds is another matter…) It makes me think that if you have any musical talent at all, just one novelty song that somehow becomes a Christmas classic would be enough to set you up for life.

That was somewhat the backstory of the movie *About a Boy* (2002). Hugh Grant's character had never had to work because his songwriter father had a hit in 1958 with a Christmas song called "Santa's Super Sleigh." The song was contrived for the movie and is satirically awful, but it would have fit pretty well in these pages if it had been seriously released.

Of course, the theory is the easy part. Actually pulling it off is something else, and you never know what will strike the public's fancy. Who could have ever predicted that "Grandma Got Run Over by a Reindeer" would still be played in the 21st century?

Up on the Housetop
Written by Benjamin R. Hanby
1864
Various Artists

This one certainly reflects its era in the list of what the kids are getting for Christmas. Even granted that there was a war going on in 1864 and expectations were rather less than would be the case now ("What? No Xbox?"), I'm still at a loss to understand why a hammer and lots of tacks would be a cool present for a little boy, unless it's just to make the rhyme work. The ball and the whip that cracks seem more like what a lad of that era might want. I've always thought Little Nell got the better present of the deal, though, since that doll sounds like it's pretty high-tech for the time.

Up on the housetop reindeer pause
Out jumps good old Santa Claus
Down through the chimney with lots of toys
All for the little ones' Christmas joys.

First comes the stocking of little Nell
Oh, dear Santa fill it well
Give her a dolly that laughs and cries
One that will open and shut her eyes

Next comes the stocking of little Will
Oh, just see what a glorious fill
Here is a hammer and lots of tacks
Also a ball and a whip that cracks

I've also found alternate versions of the last verse. One just adds a whistle to the ball and whip on the list of Little Will's loot while another makes a more substantial change:

Look in the stocking of little Bill;
Oh, just see that glorious fill!
Here is a hammer and lots of tacks,
A whistle and a ball and a set of jacks.

I can't explain the change from Will to Bill, unless it was thought that Will was dying out as a common boys' name.

But what happened to the whip that cracks? Did some well-meaning soul in more recent times think it was an inappropriate present for a little boy, since its primary purpose is to inflict pain on oppressed animals? (And would a boy even want a set of jacks? At least in my day, jacks were thought to be as much a girls' game as jumping rope.) It was a different era. In a time when the economy ran on animal-power, a whip was a regrettable necessity of life. Its primary purpose aside, a 19th Century farmboy would have thought a whip was a bully present, and gladly shown how it cracks to his admiring schoolmates at the one-room country schoolhouse before getting down to the serious business of a lunch-time game of mumblety-peg. (And imagine playing *that* on a playground today.)

Incidentally, I heard quite a bit about the songwriter, one Benjamin Hanby, in my youth. I spent my high school Senior Year in Westerville, Ohio, where Hanby had lived at one point in his life and he is still remembered as one of the town's claims to fame. My previous school years had been spent in the town that had produced the writer of the song "Dixie," so a famous local 19th Century composer was not an unfamiliar phenomenon for me as a lad.

Santa Baby

Written by Joan Javits and Philip Springer
1953
Eartha Kitt, Madonna, Taylor Swift

This cute song is a gold digger's Christmas list set to music. The original Eartha Kitt version is much to be preferred, as she coos it with class and sass. The Madonna remake sounds more like a second-rate imitation of Betty Boop.

Eartha refers to "a fifty-four convertible" on her wishlist. When the song was new, that would have been the latest model. Obviously, it would sound a little dated in a modern remake (though a recent version by Taylor Swift *does* refer to the convertible as a '54, using the original line), so the Madonna version attempts to change it to something more contemporary, but apparently without giving it any thought. The first time I heard Madonna's take on it, I thought it was "out-of-state convertible," but that may have just been my desperate attempt to make some kind of sense out of it (not that it would make a whole lot). Later re-hearings have made "outer-space" seem more likely to my ear, though it makes no particular sense, either. I checked several different song lyric websites on-line and all gave "out-of-space" (or even "auto space"), though the song may have been transcribed by people just listening to it rather than using official lyrics. What the heck would "out-of-space convertible" even *mean*!?

Trivia note: one of the songwriters, Joan Javits, was the niece of New York Senator Jacob Javits.

Winter Wonderland
Lyricist: Richard B. Smith
Composer: Felix Bernard
1934
Various Artists

From the depths of the Depression comes this exercise in "never mind if it makes any sense, it just has to rhyme."

Sleigh bells ring, are you listening,
In the lane, snow is glistening
A beautiful sight,
We're happy tonight.
Walking in a winter wonderland.

Okay, fine. The opening is the best verse in the lot. Everything adds up, the scene is established, the mood is set, and the rhymes work without having to force in some nonsense.

Gone away is the bluebird,
Here to stay is a new bird
He sings a love song,
As we go along,
Walking in a winter wonderland.

What "new bird"? Haven't all the birds that sing gone south for the winter? Unless this is a rhyme-forced metaphor for falling in love, this makes no sense! In fact, this entire verse is just irrelevant filler, adding nothing to the scene of a snow-filled landscape.

In the meadow we can build a snowman,
Then pretend that he is Parson Brown
He'll say: Are you married?
We'll say: No man,
But you can do the job when you're in town.

The verse is cute and makes the point, and the rhymes work without too much forcing. I am a little dubious about using "no man" to rhyme with "snowman," though, since it doesn't sound like something you'd say in normal conversation, especially with a parson.

Later on, we'll conspire,
As we dream by the fire
To face unafraid,
The plans that we've made,
Walking in a winter wonderland.

Conspire by the fire? Oh, what we have to do to make a rhyme. And conspire to do what? Conspire to face *plans* unafraid? This is just rhyming babble! On the syndicated *Delilah* tunes & talk radio show, one caller told how her daughter, then a toddler, misunderstood the lines as "*Later on, we'll count spiders, As they scream by the fire.*" Delilah agreed that it actually made more sense that way than in the standard version.

In the meadow we can build a snowman,
And pretend that he's a circus clown
We'll have lots of fun with Mister Snowman,
Until the other kids knock him down.

Hey, wait a minute — you already built a snowman in the meadow a couple of verses ago! Remember Parson Brown? You're repeating yourself! Well, there is some variation this time by making it a clown.

I've heard recent versions of the song that change the last line to something like, "Until the other kiddies come around." Which makes no particular sense, unless the idea is that when you've got enough kids on hand, you can go do something else, but so much for the privacy of being a couple in love walking by yourselves in a winter wonderland. And why the change, anyway? Is there a Society for the Prevention of Cruelty to Snowmen? Or did somebody just think the image of knocking over a snowman was violent and we don't want to encourage destructive behavior in our youth? One version of this I saw on-line has "Until the alligators knock him down," which I will charitably assume was a transcription error by someone who misheard it. After all, if the climate implied by a winter wonderland isn't suitable for bluebirds, it certainly isn't going to be very salubrious for the gators.

When it snows, ain't it thrilling,
Though your nose gets a chilling
We'll frolic and play, the Eskimo way,
Walking in a winter wonderland.

The song may have had some odd word choices, but it least it was grammatical and fairly high-level in tone up to now. That "ain't" out of nowhere is inconsistent with what's gone before and seems like sloppy writing, or at least an inability to sustain a mood. For that matter, "thrilling" isn't the word I'd use to describe falling snow, but I suppose nothing else would rhyme with chilling. And can you even still say "Eskimo," or does it have to be Inuit now?

You're a Mean One, Mr. Grinch

Words: Dr. Seuss
Music: Albert Hagen
1966
Thurl Ravenscroft

Though it comes from a Christmas show (the 1966 animated version of Dr. Seuss's *How the Grinch Stole Christmas*), played out of context it's a series of not at all Christmassy insults hurled at the title character by the voice of Tony the Tiger. Clever and entertaining, but a little odd by itself. Here's a sample—

You're a mean one, Mr. Grinch,
You really are a heel.
You're as cuddly as a cactus,
You're as charming as an eel,
Mr. Grinch.
You're a bad banana
With a greasy black peel.

Baby, It's Cold Outside

Written by Frank Loesser
1944
Various Artists

It may be winter-themed, but otherwise what's this one doing in the Christmas repertoire? It isn't about Christmas, it's about... well, you *know* what it's about. Are we sure we want the kids to be listening to this?

Sung as a call and response duet, the man is urging his ladyfriend not to go home since the weather is bad, but to stay the night with him. The lady sounds like she's wavering anyway and won't need much urging.

The line "Say, what's in this drink?" raises eyebrows now, like maybe he's slipped her a mickey, but in the original 1944 context it's more likely that the drink is just unexpectedly strong.

(Trivia note: According to Wikipedia, the characters are informally known as "Wolf" and "Mouse.")

My Favorite Things
Written by Rodgers & Hammerstein
1959
Diana Ross & the Supremes

While this *Sound of Music* favorite has several winter references ("warm woolen mittens," "snowflakes that stay on my nose and eye-lashes," "silver white winters that melt into spring"), it isn't particularly about winter — the opening line even refers to "Raindrops on roses" — let alone Christmas. So how did it get on the Christmas playlist? This version even has sleigh bells in the background, so somebody seems determined to make it part of the season. And not just the Supremes, since it seems to be included on a lot of Christmas albums.

The Twelve Days of Christmas
Traditional
Various Artists

There's no point in raking "The Twelve Days of Christmas" over the coals. Cackling over the absurdity of the lyrics taken literally and the impracticality of such gifts has been done to exhaustion already.

Of course, that doesn't stop somebody from computing every year how much all those gifts would cost at today's prices (assuming, of course, that the leaping lords and milking maids are hired performers rather than purchased outright, Thirteenth Amendment and all that). I forget the current total but it's rather a lot.

According to Wikipedia, "the best known English version was first printed in English in 1780 in a little book intended for children, *Mirth without Mischief*, as a Twelfth Night 'memories-and-forfeits' game, in which a leader recited a verse, each of the players repeated the verse, the leader added another verse, and so on until one of the players made a mis-take, with the player who erred having to pay a penalty, such as offering up a kiss or a sweet."

The song has evolved over time and there are numerous variations. "Four calling birds" was originally "four colly birds," for instance, from *colly* as an old word for "black," but apparently the word was causing confusion even in the 19th Century and people substituted a word they understood until the new version became standard.

Maybe the lyrics were originally just pleasant nonsense for a song that was fun to sing, and the increasing complexity of each successive verse simply made it that much harder to remember, leading to a forfeit sooner or later. If the song once had some serious symbolic intention, it has now been lost in the night of time. There have been some theories put forth about what the lyrics might mean, but as far as I know they haven't held up. I could wonder about things like if the cows come along with the eight maids a-milking and what kind of present that is to stick your true love with, but it's just trying to impose order on something that may never have had any to begin with.

So the partridge in a pear tree gets a pass this time around.

Silver Bells
Written by Jay Livingston & Ray Evans
1950
Various Artists

I have no complaints about the lyrics of this song, which simply describe pleasant Christmas scenes in a city. The only thing is, the music is so mournful that hearing it makes me think it should be a sadder song than it is. There seems to be a disconnect between the cheery words and the rather lugubrious tune.

City sidewalks busy sidewalks
Dressed in holiday style
In the air
There's a feeling
Of Christmas
Children laughing
People passing
Meeting smile after smile

I may be running it together in my mind with Roy Orbison's somewhat similar "Pretty Paper" (Willie Nelson, 1963), which is about a poor street vendor of colored pencils, paper, and ribbons. If "Silver Bells" had lyrics like these, the sorrowful tune would fit much better...

Dwight R. Decker

Crowded street, busy feet, hustle by him
Downtown shoppers, Christmas is nigh
There he sits all alone on the sidewalk
Hoping that you won't pass him by

The Christmas Waltz
Written by Sammy Cahn & Jule Styne
1954
Frank Sinatra

For the first few lines, this song has its merits...

Frosted window panes
Candles gleaming inside
Painted candy canes on the tree
Santa's on his way,
He's filled his sleigh
With things, things for you and for me

But that last line in the verse really jars with its use of the non-specific word "things," and repeated at that. "Gifts" would have been a better word, perhaps. "Thing" is just so... vague. At least "My Favorite Things" told you what the things in that song were.

It's that time of year
When the world falls in love
Every song you hear
Seems to say
Merry Christmas
May your New Year dreams come true
And this song of mine
In three quarter time
Wishes you and yours
The same thing too

"Three-quarter time"? Well, a waltz is by definition three-quarter time. The reference seems almost a little too musically technical for the lay audience, but maybe it's a knowing wink. And again there's the use of the word "thing." Three "things" in the same song are just too many things even if this thing isn't the same thing as the other things.

130

A Soldier's Silent Night
Written by James M. Schmidt
1986
Father Ted

This song (actually spoken rather than sung while "Silent Night" plays in the background) is hard to criticize since its heart is so much in the right place. Members of military families often call up the station to request it because it means a great deal to them. I just wish the commendable sentiments were served by better poetry.

'Twas the night before Christmas, he lived all alone,
In a one-bedroom house made of plaster and stone.
I had come down the chimney, with presents to give
and to see just who in this dwelling did live.

The lyrics are a bad case of the writer being pushed into odd corners by the necessity to make things rhyme, to say nothing of the bizarre situation of Santa Claus sitting by a sleeping soldier for hours on end on Christmas Eve when he should be out delivering toys. But to make fun of the garbled rhyme-driven narrative would be too cruel when the song does mean well and expresses the feelings of many people despite itself, so it also gets a pass.

Santa Claus Is Comin' to Town
Written by John Frederick Coots and Haven Gillespie
1934
Frank Sinatra & Cyndi Lauper

Now there's an unlikely duet combination, though I suspect Ol' Blue Eyes' contribution was thanks to Memorex when it was made. Best bit: Frank croons, "He sees you when you're sleeping, he knows when you're awake," and Cyndi pops up with a Brooklynish "Really?"

Incidentally, this song points up one of the troublesome parts of the Santa Claus myth: Santa as a monitor of kids' behavior and presumably observing everything they do. A grown man watching kids all the time? That's just creepy. Though parents might appreciate the idea that Junior could be dissuaded from doing something naughty for fear that some invisible spy can see him every moment of the day, it might be better to modify the myth to something like, "No, Santa doesn't watch you all the time, but he does get reports from parents, teachers, and other grown-ups, which he evaluates when he decides who's been naughty or nice." Of course, that could lead to Junior just making very sure no one's looking when he does something naughty...

Jingle Bells
Written by James Pierpont
1857
Barbra Streisand among many

This old favorite may have actually been written for Thanksgiving, though there's some dispute about that, but its winter setting brought it into the Christmas orbit. It's also thought that the word "jingle" was intended as an imperative verb.

Rhyming takes a strange turn when we get into a less often sung verse...

A day or two ago
I thought I'd take a ride
And soon Miss Fanny Bright
Was seated by my side;
The horse was lean and lank
Misfortune seemed his lot,
He got into a drifting bank
And then we got upsot.
"Upsot"?

The questioning of the word "upsot" is Streisand's amusing spoken interpolation. Presumably the word is a now forgotten dialect form of "upset." A Google search found some discussion of the matter (since the song "Jingle Bells" seems to be the only place where the word is likely to be encountered these days and people wonder about it) and even citation of a couple of 19th Century poems where the word showed up, clearly dialectical and clearly meaning "upset."

Since the rest of the song isn't in dialect, my guess is that "upsot" is there as a forced rhyme for "lot," and may have been considered an odd or humorous word choice even 150 years ago, though still quite comprehensible (like the rather jarring "ain't" in "ain't it thrilling" in "Winter Wonderland"). Now the word "upsot" in the song is just a strange rhyme, a fossil of an earlier day that merely mystifies those who run across it.

Then there's the question of exactly where Miss Fanny Bright fits in when the singer is female. Ah well, no doubt Fanny is a classmate at Miss Oglethorpe's Finishing School for Proper Young Ladies, Class of 1858, and they're just two girl chums enjoying a sleigh ride on a wintry day...

On the other hand, the Natalie Cole version changes Miss Fanny Bright to "my Mr. Right," which seems like a logical way to go for female vocalists who essay the song. Less understandable is why Natalie then says misfortune seems to be *our* lot, instead of Dobbin's. Finally, she rewrites the last line of the verse as "And then we kissed for luck," replacing a silly rhyme with no rhyme at all, while leaving unresolved the storyline of the sleigh ride and what happened as a result of the horse getting them into a drifting bank.

From what I've seen on the Web, some people confuse the song's apparently fictional Fanny Bright with Fanny Brice, the vaudeville comedienne whom Streisand portrayed in the movies *Funny Girl* and *Funny Lady,* and assume Fanny's presence in the lyrics is a modern addition and a reference to Streisand's signature role. Nope, it's just a coincidence of similar-sounding names. Fanny Bright was in the song from the start in 1857 while Fanny Brice wasn't born until 1891. Still, Streisand pronounces the name with an odd emphasis at the end of "Bright," as though to make it clear it *isn't* Brice. But since the song was done as some kind of whimsy (its title has a question mark at the end — "Jingle Bells?" — and it's sung unnaturally fast, perhaps as a stunt), not calling the lady in the song Fanny Brice after all seems like an opportunity for a joke that shouldn't have gone untouched.

To my surprise, a look online turned up two additional verses of the song that I didn't even know existed. They must be seldom or never sung in the present century.

It's Beginning to Look a Lot Like Christmas
Meredith Willson
1951
Various Artists

This modern-era standard was written by the *Music Man* man.

It's beginning to look a lot like Christmas
Toys in ev'ry store
But the prettiest sight to see
Is the holly that will be
On your own front door

A pair of hopalong boots and a pistol that shoots
Is the wish of Barney and Ben
Dolls that will talk and will go for a walk
Is the hope of Janice and Jen
And Mom and Dad can hardly wait for school to start again.

The question here is what the heck are those "hopalong boots" that Barney and Ben want. Could this be a now forgotten period reference, and forever to be a mystery to future generations of children? That is, in 1951, Western star Bill Boyd, otherwise known as Hopalong Cassidy, was the popular cowboy hero of that era's generation of little boys. Is this perhaps the key to the mystery?

As for the dolls that Janice and Jen want, they show how far doll-making technology had come from what Little Nell found in her stocking back in 1864 in "Up on the Housetop."

The Little Drummer Boy
Written by Katherine Kennicott Davis & Harry Simeone
1941, 1958
Harry Simeone Chorale

Originally published in 1941 under the name "Carol of the Drum," this song became a breakout hit in 1958 as "The Little Drummer Boy" performed by an ad hoc group called the Harry Simeone Chorale. The name makes me think of hairy simians in a corral, but Harry Simeone was a quite real composer, conductor, and arranger. Since he arranged the hit version of the song, he demanded co-credit for it even though he didn't actually write it. I certainly hope the old lady music teacher at Wellesley College who did write it years before saw some money from it.

I can't say the song is exactly one of my faves. It's sung very nearly *a capella*, one chorus singing the high notes and the male chorus doing the drumbeat. With just a chime ringing now and then, it seems like a bleak and empty musical landscape to me.

For one friend of mine, though, it's very different. He was seven at Christmas time in 1958, and he once told me that he recalls lying on the floor in his dark living room and looking at the lighted Christmas tree while the song was playing on the radio. Being seven, he imagined the male chorus as consisting of cartoon cats all resembling Oil Can Harry, the dapperly dressed villain of *Mighty Mouse* cartoons. Ever since, he said, hearing the song takes him back to that childhood moment, and he remembers the living room and its furniture, his parents' voices in the next room, being happy that he didn't have to go back to school until after New Year's, looking forward to Christmas Day right around the corner...

Many years later, I ran across a compilation of Christmas songs on CD that included that song. I recalled my old pal saying that he didn't have a copy, so I bought it on a whim and sent it to him. I didn't realize he was going through a bad patch right then, and he said later that getting the CD completely out of the blue like that was a wonderful surprise. He played the song about seven or eight times straight just about in tears, and for a moment or two it did take him back to a time when he was young and life was simple. I hadn't planned it that way, but it was a little pick-me-up right when he needed one.

I think that's true for a lot of us. Christmas songs were part of our childhoods, and we heard them every year when we were most impressionable. Hearing them again jogs our memories of times long gone. "The Little Drummer Boy" may not do it for me, but there are a couple that could make me a bit misty.

Last Christmas
Written by George Michael
1984
Various Artists from Taylor Swift to Sailor Mars

This song only dates back to 1984 when it was released as a pop single by the duo Wham!, but it has been covered by numerous artists since and looks to be gaining a place as a permanent part of the Christmas scene. The somewhat melancholy lyrics are more about a failed romance than about Christmas, though, using the annual holiday as both a special occasion when love blooms and a marker for the passage of a year. One rumor has it that the song was originally written with Easter as the milestone holiday but someone realized that it would probably sell better as a Christmas song. Whoever did the realizing seems to have been exactly right, given the song's enduring popularity.

I hadn't really noticed the song until I heard the *Glee* TV cast version on the overhead speaker at a drugstore one Yuletide season and realized I rather liked at least that rendition. Since the performers weren't identified, it took some detective work to track it down, but *Glee* was hot that year and I had a fair idea of the likely source. Other versions, like the original one by Wham!, or by Taylor Swift or Sailor Mars (actually Michie Tomizawa, the Japanese voice artist for Sailor Mars in the anime series *Sailor Moon*), haven't appealed to me nearly as much, but the *Glee* kids sing their hearts out and give it a certain intensity.

Sleigh Ride

Leroy Anderson
1948
Lyrics by Mitchell Parrish added in 1950
Various Artists

This song began as an instrumental piece painting a sound picture of the title excursion, composed by Leroy Anderson (who specialized in novelty orchestral pieces and is also known for "The Syncopated Clock" and "The Typewriter"), with the lyrics added later by other hands as something of an afterthought. It describes much the same situation as "Jingle Bells," but this sleigh ride fortunately ends with a party instead of a traffic accident. The song is fine as long it stays in the sleigh, but things get a little off-track with the party at Farmer Gray's.

There's a birthday party at the home of Farmer Gray
It'll be the perfect ending of a perfect day

Why a *birthday* party, exactly? The song doesn't even mention Christmas but it has become a seasonal standard solely because of the winter theme. Making it a Christmas party at Farmer Gray's would have really clinched the deal. Variants exist, however: The Carpenters' version does change it to a Christmas party in a line sung by none other than ex-Mouseketeer Cubby O'Brien, while it's still a birthday party when others have at it.

There's a happy feeling nothing in the world can buy
When they pass around the coffee and the pumpkin pie

I suppose the intention with these lines was to express a sense of warm conviviality among friends, but they just seem like a letdown when that great feeling promised in the first line turns out to be nothing more than coffee and pie in the second.

It'll nearly be like a picture print by Currier and Ives
These wonderful things are the things we remember
all through our lives!

The reference to Currier & Ives may already need a footnote to explain it to recent generations. Currier & Ives was a firm that sold vast numbers of lithographs of colored drawings of popular and sentimental scenes, inexpensive art for the masses that hung on half the walls in America during the 19th Century. While I can easily imagine a print showing a horse-drawn sleigh coursing through the snow (because I've actually seen prints like that), the lyrics seem to imply that what seems like a scene from an antique picture is the coffee and pie being passed around to the guests in Farmer Gray's parlor. Which seems a little dull for a print. Did the Currier & Ives line get put in the wrong verse?

Maybe it's the result of hearing it so often on the radio, but I find myself particularly fond of Debbie Gibson's version of this song. It might be because of the endearing (and annoying at the same time) way she pronounces "pumpkin pahh"...

Snoopy's Christmas
Written by George David Weiss, Hugo & Luigi
1967
The Royal Guardsman

Just another follow-up to the original novelty song "Snoopy vs. the Red Baron" of 1966, this is the one that's remembered and still played.

Probably unintentionally, this little fantasy of the cartoon canine World War I flying ace unexpectedly sharing a brief Christmas toast with his archenemy, the Red Baron, dimly reflects an actual historical event. That is, during Christmas, 1914, when the British Army was facing the German Army along the Western Front, there was an unplanned lull in the fighting in some places and men on both sides took a break from trying to kill each other to meet in an impromptu truce and celebrate Christmas together. For a moment, the line about "peace on Earth and goodwill to men" really meant something. Then it was back to business as usual, and the slaughter went on for years.

But for that one moment... Like the Red Baron said (in the song, anyway), "Merry Christmas, *mein Friend!*"

That concludes this survey of a random assortment of Christmas songs. A few more could have been included, but then we would have been getting into the territory of songs I *really* dislike, and my bilious commentary would have spoiled what little Christmas cheer is left after the foregoing. So let's close out instead with something I actually do like.

After all the above critical commentary on song lyrics, I'm starting to think that *The Ventures Christmas Album* (1965) is my favorite Christmas album of all time. The Ventures being an instrumental group (you might call them my unsung heroes), there aren't any lyrics *at all* on that album!

Except, I must admit, the words "silver bells" as a refrain on the song of the same name, produced by some manner of musical wizardry — steel guitar? — instead of by a human voice.

Purists might complain the Ventures hoked up Christmas favorites by playing them in the styles of their own songs, like opening "Sleigh Ride" with the intro to "Walk Don't Run," or adding riffs from other mid-'60s songs (is that "I Feel Fine" mixed with "Rudolph the Red-Nosed Reindeer"? and the mix of "Tequila" with "Frosty the Snowman" is certainly thinking outside the box), but the thirteen-year-old boy still within me who first bought that album likes them a little hokey.

But aren't a lot of Christmas songs like that, like the ones I took a look at above? Hokey, I mean? And it's not even a bad thing? Most of the year we consider ourselves quite the sophisticates in our musical tastes, but for a few weeks in December we let our inner little kid out to indulge in sentiment and sleigh bells. That's how we like our old favorites, even, sometimes, when there's more rhyme than reason in the lyrics...

About the Author

Dwight R. Decker was born in Ohio, which is why so many of his stories are set in the Buckeye State. After keeping one step ahead of the authorities by living variously in New York, Los Angeles, and Phoenix, he currently hangs his hat in the Chicago area. For quite a few years, he earned his daily crust as a technical writer in the telecommunications industry while also laboring on occasion as a free-lance translator of comics and science fiction. He now has the time to devote to books like this one, with more to come.

Also Available

Novels & Short Stories
by Dwight R. Decker

Pleistocene Junior High

An entire middle school full of kids winds up 30,000 years in the past. Meanwhile, one boy holds the key to their return in the palm of his hand. Literally.

A Moon of Their Own

Trapped in an orbiting theme park gone mad, 15-year-old Ronn Evans and his cousins have to find a way back to Earth before they're marooned there forever.

Some Other Shore

Six lighthearted short stories exploring the odder reaches of fantasy and science fiction. Hänsel and Gretel made real, pseudo-time travel, mermaids (two different kinds!), bogus UFOs and a genuine alien... and something more.

A Dream Flying

An ordinary boy living in Ordinaryville, he dreamed of being able to fly like Superman. Then one day, his fantasy became his destiny, and nothing was ever very ordinary again.

Dancing with the Squirrels: Tales from Comics Fandom and Beyond

New and old stories featuring the misadventures of comic-book fans. The fictional locales range from a small town in Illinois to Los Angeles and even England, but the strangest story of all is set in Cincinnati... and happens to be perfectly true! (And led directly to the publication of *The Crackpot* — see next page.)

Coming Distractions

The Napoleon of Time

In a near-infinity of alternate worlds, two college instructors from different centuries find each other in 1912 Poughkeepsie — and in her rush to join him, she *would* have to book passage on the most famous doomed ship of all time.

Coming soon.

Man and Astroman

Matt Dawson is a young physicist caught up in an experiment gone wrong, finding himself with super-powers in a parallel world much like ours but somehow a little wacky and seemingly stuck in 1963. Meanwhile, a local hero called Astroman has mysteriously disappeared, and only Matt can find out what happened to him. Add in a little romance with Astrogirl and a trip through space and time to a doomed planet, and the result is an homage to a fondly remembered comic-book series with a touch of pulp space adventure.

Coming soon.

Rendezvous in Sarajevo

If you found out you were destined to die in World War I, wouldn't you try to stop it before it started? Even if the Paratemporal History Institute thinks changing history corrupts the data and is out to stop *you*?

Coming soon.

Collections & Translations
Edited by DRD

The Crackpot and other twisted tales of greedy fans and collectors
by John E. Stockman

Between 1962 and 1979, the reclusive Mr. Stockman wrote some of the wackiest stories ever, recounting the strange antics of deranged comic-book collectors and obsessed fans of the author Edgar Rice Burroughs. Eight of his best stories have been rescued from the crumbling mimeographed pages of the legendary (and only too aptly named) fanzine *Tales of Torment*, including many of Stockman's own illustrations. With historical notes and commentary, published by Ramble House.

Flying Fish "Prometheus"
   by Vilhelm Bergsøe
      Jules Verne-style science fiction first published in Danish in 1870 and now translated into English. A journey from Denmark to Central America by airship in the far future year of 1969 goes terribly wrong. With translation notes, maps, vintage illustration, and historical background.

The Speedy Journey
   by Eberhard Christian Kindermann
      Published in German in 1744 and never before translated, this is the first fictional account of a trip to Mars (or at least somewhere close by). Historical and literary detective work puts together an often amusing background story that has mostly been missed until now. Was Kindermann a prophetic visionary or one of the all-time great cranks — or a little of both? With notes, new and vintage illustrations, and historical essays.

Available from the usual on-line sources, including the mail-order retailer that conducts its trade under the name of a mighty South American river. For the thrifty reader reluctant to pay for ink, glue, and paper, some of the books can be obtained in the form of their pure spiritual essence as Kindle e-book editions. Check book listings for availability.